Moods

Also by Yoel Hoffmann

FROM NEW DIRECTIONS

Bernhard

The Christ of Fish

Curriculum Vitae

The Heart Is Katmandu

Katschen & The Book of Joseph

The Shunra and the Schmetterling

MOODS

Yoel Hoffmann

translated by Peter Cole

A NEW DIRECTIONS PAPERBOOK

Moods is published by arrangement with the Keter Publishing House and
the Harris / Elon Agency of Israel.

First published as a New Directions Paperbook (NDP1306) in 2015
Manufactured in the United States of America
New Directions Books are printed on acid-free paper
Design by Erik Rieselbach.

Library of Congress Cataloging-in-Publication Data
Hoffmann, Yoel.
[Matsve ruah. English]
Moods / Yoel Hoffmann ; translated by Peter Cole.
pages cm
Originally published as: Matsve ruah. Yerushalayim : Keter, c2010.
ISBN 978-0-8112-2382-9 (alk. paper)
1. Psychological fiction. 2. Experimental fiction, Jewish.
I. Cole, Peter, 1957– translator. II. Title.
PJ5054.H6319M3713 2015
892.43'6—dc23   2015001270

10 9 8 7 6 5 4 3 2

New Directions Books are published for James Laughlin
by New Directions Publishing Corporation
80 Eighth Avenue, New York 10011

MOODS

[1]

Ever since finishing my last book, I've been thinking of
how to begin the next one.

Beginning is everything and needs to contain, like the
seed of a tree, the work as a whole.

And so, what I see is the figure of a man descending
(from the sidewalk?) five or six steps to a basement apartment, and he's halfway there.

I know it's a love story. And maybe there's a woman in
the basement apartment. It's probably November.

[2]

I remember things that happened in an empty building
(which is to say, one they hadn't yet finished building) in
Ramat Gan, in the fifties.

Then too (as now) legs were the principal thing. The
world was full of legs of all sorts and there was movement in space. Someone—Ezra Danischevsky—said to
me once: I want to be an elevator repairman (you can
imagine the motion and its various directions).

In that (empty) building, a woman who's now seventy-
four (if she's not dead) took off her dress.

[3]

And so his name—that of the man going down the steps—is, most likely, Nehemiah. Not because it's true, but because of that combination of sounds—"his name" and "is … Nehemiah," and because of its implicit acknowledgment of God, without whom perhaps the world exists, though He is the master of words.

It's hard to call a woman by name because Nothingness swallows everything, and the one contains the many, although, in other respects, highly partial, her name is possibly Hermione.

A policeman or two pass on the street and their legs are now on an imaginary plane above which sits the head of a man.

After my father died, I spritzed his deodorant into my armpits for three or four months. It smelled like musk.

My father also had a Schaffhausen watch, which wasn't removed even when he fell into a coma.

[4]

I too (Yoel Hoffmann, that is) once went like that down steps to a place where a French woman waited.

I'd trailed her from the Metro stop to the building's entrance, and since she looked at me and twirled the key on her finger suggestively, I followed her down to the basement apartment.

Maybe the scene with Nehemiah is only a memory of *this* scene, and what I did, he'll do as well.

Bookstores hold an infinite number of memories like these, but only a few speak in praise of whores.

[5]

The act of love gives birth to blue birds, just as once we could walk through a door without having to open it. Girls set entire streets on fire. Kiosks floated into the air. People wailed as though in distress, but perfumed vapors rose from their lips.

In the room, the French woman held out a hand (one of the two she had) and took the thousand-franc bill, as one takes the wine and wafer from a priest.

[6]

A forty-watt bulb (elsewhere I've called it an electric pear) lit up the bed but the picture of the Virgin (and Child) stood outside the cone of light like an omen. Sometimes one sees a sign, like ARLOSOROFF STREET, and goes there, and in fact the street's just like that.

The French woman pulled the dress up over her head and stood there utterly naked (I remember an accountant who always said, "Bottom line—" which is to say, "net")— no bra, no panties.

[7]

Literature's so pathetic. We peddle fabric with a sun painted on it and no one even looks up.

The bed. Thighs. The backside. A person who wants to know the flesh had best bite into his finger. Only then will he know.

And he should see my Aunt Edith. How she fell into herself, in the wheelchair, until her mouth sank into her jaw and her jaw sank into her chest and still she said— time after time, until she died—*noch* (which is to say, "more").

[8]

The woman was maybe forty and had (she said) a child in the country. The act of love she undertook as one turns the pages of a newspaper (*Le Figaro*, for example).

Undoubtedly. She thought of other things during intercourse. Maybe she saw a woman in the village calling her son: Claude, Claude. Or the candles that one lights at church. In any event, she held me, as the Virgin in the picture holds the Child, and sighed.

[9]

I could write about how the Bible that the principal gave me at the end of eighth grade saved my life (it was in the pocket of my army vest and the bullet went into it up to the Book of Nehemiah) or, how, as though in an American movie, I went to the wedding of a girl I was in love with once and at the last minute etcetera. Which is to say, a bona fide story with plot twists and intrigue and an ending cut off like a salami (to keep it modern).

Books like those have at least three hundred and twenty eight pages, and in the end mobs of people running around you like holograms.

But I can't, because of the turquoise sunbirds.

[10]

And because of the picture (*The Potato Eaters*) Van Gogh painted maybe some thirty times, each time the light falling in a different manner.

Which makes me think of the potatoes at the Austrian old age home in Ramat Gan.

My Aunt Edith and Francesca, my stepmother, saw these potatoes on blue plastic plates and sometimes their forks sparkled in the light of the light. Not to mention Mr. Cohen, who sat at another table and was a hundred years old.

As in the chorus of Beethoven's Ninth, there wasn't a single potato that wasn't in its proper place.

[11]

Ezra Danischevsky did indeed become an elevator repairman, but in Los Angeles. He summoned, so I heard, Haim Gluzman, and the two of them installed elevators there.

You're walking horizontally and suddenly you're lifted along a vertical axis. After a while, you descend the vertical axis and go back to walking horizontally. Sometimes you're parallel to the ground (that is, your entire body is horizontal), as when making love.

[12]

The French woman washed below her navel in the bidet and talked about Algiers, which needed (like her) to be

French. Outside it was raining, and maybe love was born at the sight of her toes.

How many books have I written in order to conceal that sight, and here, at last, it's revealed. I do now what I didn't do then, and one by one I kiss them. From the little toe on her right foot up to the big one, and from the big toe on her left down to the little one. If there were hair on my head it would fall across the sole of her foot. May His great Name be exalted and sanctified.

[13]

My stepmother Francesca called the ground *Boden*. The two of us walked across the ground but, because of this other name, it (the ground) carried her differently.

There was a Mrs. Minoff, whose silk stockings every so often would develop a run (in Hebrew then they called it a "train"). Mrs. Minoff and my stepmother Francesca exchanged romance novels (in German), and sometimes they were joined in this by Mrs. Shtiasny, whose husband was Italian.

Mrs. Shtiasny's Italian husband died suddenly in a dentist's waiting room. The three (namely, Francesca, my stepmother, Mrs. Minoff, and Mrs. Shtiasny) stood there a good long while at the cemetery by the door to the room where the corpses are washed. My stepmother Francesca finally went in and when she came out she looked at Mrs. Shtiasny and said: Nah Yah.

[14]

In popular parlance people say "don't make yourself out to be" this or that, but we're always making ourselves out to be something. Only the blood flows without being told where to go (if readers would like a fine Merlot, they should look into Yiron wines).

There's no longer any limit to the things that I (from here on in I'll say "we," out of embarrassment) are able to say. We can make soup from ghosts (which is to say, we can say that). We can push nails in from the wrong end. We know the difference between ourselves and others. Which is to say, others are imprisoned within their skin. We guess, for years. Paint mezuzahs. Steep tea. Grind. Herd. Toast. And on and on. We can say a single thing an infinite number of times.

We also ask for forgiveness. From the widow. From the air-conditioner technician. From the saleswoman at the Castro store.

[15]

It's strange that the German word for widow is *Witwe.* Imagine that a man might say: I saw a *Witwe.* No one would think he had seen a widow.

I remember the smells in the widow's home. The smell of the old suitcase over the closet. The smell of the sewing machine (which stood in the middle of the room precisely), and the smell of the pillows.

As in other books that speak of widows, so too the widow in this one hung a picture of her dead husband on the wall.

[16]

If we had to introduce her as a character we could say she was wide like the woman doctor at the end of Ya'akov Shabtai's novel. Scenes of distant gardens, and she was kneeling.

Which brings to mind St. Ignatius of Padova, who, in the thirteenth century, sailed on a fishing boat to Alexandria, where (through miraculous acts) he saved a hundred Muslim women.

St. Ignatius, most likely, loathed the flesh, but when he blessed the women (each in turn), prayers rose up from them.

[17]

If you walked the length of the Hebrew Encyclopedia you'd get to a balcony from which you could see the sea. Sometimes we stood there all alone because the widow was speaking on the telephone, or taking a bath.

What broke our hearts was the volume of supplemental entries. We saw in our mind's eye how the widow would look for corrections there, and also for updates to all the other volumes, and she could hardly bear the fragments of the moon above Tel Aviv. Or else she'd go into the kitchen and sit, and the teakettle would suddenly shriek.

[18]

We don't know if this book will make it into print, but all of a sudden we've understood that authors breathe.

Haim Be'er is breathing, and Amos Oz is breathing, and we too are taking breaths. The heart, it's true, can skip a beat, but one can't skip a breath or breathe backward— only chronologically. Many things are bound so deeply, and we still haven't spoken of air and photosynthesis, etcetera.

And it happens that a writer can die before he's completed a word (chinaberry, for instance), or that he might pass away between books and the posthumous book won't be written.

[19]

What exactly the widow was thinking no one ever knew. Most likely she thought we'd move into her apartment, and that in due course she'd remarry.

These things become clear in memory as well, for instance, that once she said something that had to do with it being two years since that day, and that she'd asked to have new tiles put in or had moved the Persian rug from its place. And the grocery store beneath her apartment, which had rolls by six-thirty in the morning. But mostly seeing her there on all fours, her knees on the ground and the palms of her hands on the floor.

[20]

One can write in a figurative fashion and one can write abstractly. But you'll have to ask the academicians how to distinguish between the two.

The cattle prod (our Bible teachers told us about) is, for example, abstract, but the number eight is figurative without a doubt.

A week ago at Café Henrietta (at 186 Arlosoroff Street) I saw a man whose name was apparently Chedorlaomer. In matters like these the elements mix. In any event, it's wise to aim at the middle ground between the two: that's where mercy is.

[21]

The Schaffhausen watch on my father's wrist when he died held within it tiny springs (not what they put in watches today) and nevertheless its hands displayed the correct time.

It's possible to see how, with very fine tweezers, the Swiss watchmaker would take such a spring from the table. The Swiss man himself is made of such springs, even if they don't work as they should within him.

The men who held these springs are already dead, or very old, and their wives have died as well. Picture the wife of a watchmaker. How she places a bowl of beets on the table.

[22]

Now we're experiencing pain in the chest and don't remember if the heart is on the right side or the left. The night is deep and the (digital) clock shows that it's two-thirty.

We're thinking of networks. Spider webs. A chain of shoe stores. Or fishermen's nets and networks that the eyes can't see.

And childhood loves. How we waited each morning for the girl who sat on the third bench and all the halls in the school led to her. She came through our heart as though it were the Mandelbaum Gate, but the heart (of flesh) was smaller then because we were children.

Now the butcher shops are closed, and the butchers are sleeping in their large beds. May God watch over them and their wives.

[23]

Because he has only a single life (though "life" in Hebrew is plural—*hayyim*), a person always returns to the same things.

The girl in third grade—her name wasn't what we said it was in another book. In fact we loved two girls at once. The other one was in 3-G, and her homeroom teacher was Yitzhak Karton (penultimate stress), but we've forgotten her name.

In the schoolyard there were faucets, and all the girls drank from them, and we could see all sorts of braids like a book that's being translated into many languages.

[24]

Our heart breaks at the sight of fire hydrants, or words like *home cooking*.

How many grocers we've seen (at stores) and we've never once placed our hand on their head as the Pope might. Some of them came from Auschwitz, and now they're dead, and we just said white bread, or two hundred grams of cheese, and left the mailboxes as they were and didn't kneel before them or lift up our hands.

We said "we need to call the plumber," as though the power of speech were an ordinary matter.

[25]

Later on, Bracha Kalvari asked us to undo her bra, and we went behind her like St. Francis of Brindisi, who wandered through graveyards and looked at the tombstones only from the side that was smooth.

And there was Nehamah Nehamah. The absolute parity between her first name and last seemed to determine that she would surrender her body into the hands of others as well.

But those were the days of Billie Holiday, and so every act of what we called petting trailed a saxophone's echo.

[26]

This book barely mentions men but we owe several (from back then) a slap.

Now it's hard to settle such accounts. We could hire a private eye to find out where they live, but then we'd be faced with men who bear almost no resemblance to who they were. And we today are different too, and undoubtedly these old men would have trouble remembering us.

And we could settle up with the teachers as well, but they're dead, and most likely are teaching others who have died.

[27]

Joy. Breakers. A laughing dove. Tea bags. Bacchanalia. Miscarriage of justice. Thoughts. A hip's rise. Pay stubs. Paso doble. Armageddon. Six of. Bilateralism. Oxymoron. Marble. Raspberry juice. Gustav the Great. Teeth. Serbonian Bog. Concubine. Copper mines. Vayzata. Irkutsk. Osmosis. Allies. Schopenhauer. Salmon, etcetera.

Yes. And we've forgotten runnels.

[28]

Rossini (the classical station's saying just now) was plagued by backaches in 1842.

In Japanese the back is *senaka*. *Senaka*, we think, is the perfect word for it. More accurate than, for instance, *back*, or *Rücken*.

They pressed the back of the crucified one against the cross (as we once pressed Penina Tuchner against the kitchen cabinet) and the men below saw only his chest. But the back bore the brunt of the torment because it was pressed against the boards.

[29]

I had a dream: We're (which is to say, I'm) alone at an airport. But the monitor's showing departures only. Which is to say, planes at that airport only take off.

If we could surround everything with words (as others do), we would. But we see just a very little. The extent of things blends into the surrounding space.

Once we went to a psychoanalyst and understood that she hated her husband.

[30]

In autumn the walls of the house grow cold. You listen to
Billie Holiday and it seems you're hearing a Bach Passion.

You think about the soul of a hen. How she stares and
sees things, like a wheelbarrow or a pitchfork. And about
the soul of a horse.

Suddenly you ask yourself what turpentine is. You're
thinking: I'm a man. What of it?

For all we've said in a contorted fashion, we ask forgiveness. When we talked about the pancreas and the circuits
of heaven and didn't know what children know who hide
their faces in their hands and shout: "Ready or not, here
I come."

[31]

What slayed us was high heels. The vertical line of the leg
and also at times (when the shoes were mules) the heel.

We saw legs like those at the end of Allenby Street next
to the Opera House. On one side of the street was an iron
railing and on the other were gambling joints of various
sorts. Other writers would certainly describe the whores
quite well, and also the gulls.

Whoever went there went there. Some would lean against the railing and look toward the sea, and sometimes they saw (as one sees a shooting star) a gull die and fall into the water.

[32]

We hear a name like *Mittelpunkt*, which means a point in the middle.

Since space is infinite there is no point in the middle of the world, and therefore these people (called Mittelpunkt) are themselves that point in the middle. If we extend lines in every direction from where they are, these lines would be equal in length.

My Aunt Edith was afraid that the ground would smother her. But several saints (so we heard) lay down in coffins while they were still alive. They pointed their bodies in the right direction but their spirits floated and they thought (in the dark of the coffin) things like, Where's that brown shawl?

[33]

We'd like to use the phrase *hard times*. To say, for instance, because of the hard times I slept fitfully and my mind wandered. A wandering mind is a marvelous sight.

During the summer you can see people sitting at cafés. Their upper bodies are properly cast (like busts of composers we put on pianos). But beneath the tables you see their toes, and some are afflicted with mycosis.

From Aunt Edith we ask forgiveness for our not having read the letters she left behind.

[34]

Old telephones are preserved in memories. The voice that emerged from the receiver frightened us. We couldn't understand where the face had gone.

Now in phones you can see faces that are far away. But the sadness is greater by a factor of seven precisely because you see them.

If we could bring Aunt Edith back, we would. Even to the time when she had to sit in a wheelchair. She'd be amazed by the sight of the Azrieli skyscraper in Tel Aviv.

[35]

We can talk about a certain man's life and the people who were bound to him because people were bound to us as well.

There was a radio repairman who was bound to us during the days when radios were made of lamps. And Uncle Zoltan, who heard the symphony's concerts (on the radio), and Mr. Yaar, who sold shoes, and so on and so on.

That is to say, we thought they were bound to us, and they thought we were bound to them. The whole thing's very complicated, as a post office clerk, Rahamim Kadosh (whom we've written of elsewhere), once said: It's been ages since I've seen you, and you haven't seen me either.

[36]

Uncle Zoltan also conducted the concert he heard on the radio because he knew how to read what people call scores. Generally speaking. He was extremely learned, and knew the grammatical structures of some thirty languages.

And even though he was a doctor at the Labor Union Clinic on Zamenhoff Street, and saw a great many people there, when people came to his home (largely to visit Aunt Edith) he'd lock himself in the bathroom and not come out until they were gone.

He was bound to Aunt Edith and she was bound to him, out of loneliness. Each would walk from here to there all alone and come back to an empty home. But because each was bound to the other they were able to ring the doorbell.

And someone opens the door for us too, and for this we thank God (and He, when you give it some thought, is always alone).

[37]

My other uncle, my father Andreas's brother—his name was Laudislaus—was also a doctor. He knew how to wiggle his ears, like an elephant, though his diagnoses were often wrong.

We too inherited this gift from our forebears, and there's a good chance that we are the only author who can wiggle his ears like that. We can also bend our thumb all the way back to our wrist.

We've already written in another book about the donkey that Uncle Laudislaus received from the clinic (because there weren't any roads in Ramat Gan at the time). Since then we've seen donkeys and she-asses in all sorts of places, and we can say that there are no lovelier eyelashes than those of a donkey (or a she-ass).

[38]

Yesterday the tax authorities put a block on our salary. Not because of any debt, but because of a dispute over when our return needed to be filed.

We called wherever we called and sent faxes to various places, but without a doubt, because of it all, something slipped our minds. If we had a union or league (as of nations), thirty or forty readers would have waved cardboard signs before a government building.

We've heard there are writers who can't, as we say, "finish the month" and pay their bills. We too have trouble when it comes to finishing the month. We also have trouble starting it, as feelings are always troubling our heart. The feeling of things past. Of sights. And things we've lost. Of night.

We send up a prayer that we won't be so needy.

[39]

The air over Nahariya is full of crows. These small black people know a thing or two that people below do not. We hear them as one hears a large synagogue.

Sometimes a crow comes down between the tables at a café and sees the urologist from the Clinic, or a woman named Aviva.

But at dusk, all fly up from the tops of the eucalyptus trees, like a man who can't remember if he's taken off his socks, drunk at the sight of the weakening sun.

[40]

Because of this dispute with the authorities we've sought out, in Nahariya, a man who is also an accountant. His name is Tugenhauft, which means (we think) "given to sorrow." We can already see the sorrow in the stairwell.

Ernst Tugenhauft has us sit in a chair and we open books before him. In the meantime, the sun has already set and the crows (so we hear) have returned to the trees. And we (which is to say Ernst Tugenhauft and I) are crows on a lower plane. Within the large room our bodies are gradually darkening and our mouths grow long.

[41]

In the end, the authorities responded to Ernst Tugenhauft and the deadline for the return was extended, but now our blood pressure isn't right and we need to lower the upper number.

But the blood is pressing as it always has against the tubes beneath the flesh. It's figuring out how to break through to the blood that's beyond us, and sometimes it breaks though the tubes and strikes against the skull.

People don't know that once there was a man named Buxtehude. His name comes to mind because of the mystery words embody. One could say "the blood of Ernst Tugenhauft," but it isn't possible to say (which is to say, one can say but not think) the words "the blood of Buxtehude."

[42]

It's been ages since we've spoken of beautiful things.

We remember how beautiful the widow was, although by most people's standards her face was ugly. We weren't, however, bound to her at all because she remained within herself, as she was, only up to the borders where the air begins.

If we were Catholic, we'd go to the priest and confess before him that we haven't received with true submission the divine design and we've sought for ourselves empty space.

[43]

We remember how beautiful Uncle Zoltan was. And how beautiful our stepmother Francesca was (her maiden name was Manheim). They too were precisely what they were, but then, when we were children, we only wanted solid forms.

We might sketch out episodes but we can't. We've forgotten adjectives and adverbs and we remember (like the mentally disabled) just first names.

It's only right that we should read the phone book as we read Scripture.

[44]

A certain sheikh from a Sufi sect saw that the time to pray had come. He started to rise from his pallet and was just about to go to the mosque. But since a cat was sleeping on the sleeve of his cloak, he cut off the sleeve and went to pray with his one arm covered and the other exposed.

The cat is already dead, and the sheikh too has passed away, but year after year tens of thousands of pilgrims prostrate themselves before this sleeve. Some crawl on their bellies (like the Christians who come to Fatima, in Portugal, to the grave of the child-shepherds who saw the Holy Virgin in the sky) from the edge of town and across the spice market up to the mosque where the sleeve is preserved.

Hence the injunction, Be a sleeve to the world. If the woman beside you is sleeping and her head is on your arm and you need to get up and go to the bathroom you very carefully have to place her head on the pillow beside you (how tempting it is to say you have to cut off your arm) just so you won't wake her.

[45]

Penina Tuchner we loved like the Twin Towers, especially when they were burning. If her bra were preserved in a museum, we'd go there and break the display-case glass.

How she'd say "Shalom," with that first syllable precisely placed between *s* and *sh*. Generally. She pronounced words like a swan sailing along on the Thames, next to the hotels. You could see her throat through her neck.

We remember that she lived at 15 Tribes of Israel Street, on the third floor. On the first (we remember) there lived people whose names were Kalantar and people whose names were Yesharim. On the second floor were people whose names were Laufer, and on the third (facing Tuchner) lived a man named Fabricant.

[46]

Mrs. Tuchner (Penina's mother) used to put soup pots on the windowsill. We remember that a large pot came between us and our view of the apartment across the way.

When we ate (Mr. Tuchner would eat with us too), Mrs. Tuchner would walk from the table to the kitchen and back. Mr. Tuchner's eyeglasses would fog up with vapors and he would remove them every so often and wipe the lenses with the tablecloth.

We thought to ourselves then that they (which is to say, Mr. and Mrs. Tuchner) brought a baby girl into the world and waited until she grew up and now we take off all of her clothes.

[47]

We've heard that physicists are searching for a tiny particle that they can't find and therefore they've built an enormous tunnel in Switzerland.

We too from time to time lose a breadcrumb, but usually we find it under the table. My stepmother Francesca lost an imitation pearl once and after a while she found it between the sheets.

Happy are people who lack only a tiny particle. Sometimes we lose what seems like half the world or even two thirds of it, and the part that's left is a blackish-yellow like the streets of Europe in the nineteenth century, when they'd light the lamps with gas.

[48]

At times like these only a dog can diagnose the problem. He places his head on our knees and sends us healing powers. And this (that is, the dog's soul) is one of the great mysteries about which one can't write in books.

We remember all the dogs that were bound to us. Their souls are now in heaven. Their paws are preserved in the great Pantheon of the World Spirit.

And this is the schedule of buses departing from Nahariya to Ma'alot: 5:15, 6:30, 6:45, 7:00, 7:20, 7:45, 8:30, 11:30, 13:30, 16:00, 18:25, 19:30, and the last one is at 20:35.

[49]

And now it's only fitting that we should talk about the shopkeeper and the dog.

Every day Mr. Hirsch would slice up a large chunk of cheese. His hand went up and down as he sliced, and therefore we couldn't see if the number on his arm and the number on the arm of his wife were in sequence.

Mr. Hirsch also taught us to distinguish between white bread and dark bread. They don't bake loaves like that any longer. But then they'd cut three small grooves into the outer crust of the white bread.

The dog would always lie by the door to the grocery store and growl. Perhaps he saw in his mind's eye a pot

roast (or something called ratatouille) and was angry that
he couldn't smell what was cooking.

[50]

Next to the grocery store was a shop that belonged to a
tailor named Leopold. And after that was a store called
My Book, where they sold books and stationery supplies.

The movements in the grocery store were, on the whole,
vertical (which is to say they went from top to bottom).
At the tailor's the movement was lateral (which is to say,
horizontal—on account of the line drawn in the air by the
needle and thread). And at My Book the movement was
crosshatched. On the pavement in front of the stores the
children played with small glass marbles.

Once the tailor whose name was Leopold left the
store and chased all the children away. But the children
came back and some of them even pressed their noses
against the window of the shop in order to see the tailor's
dummy.

[51]

At the bookstore called My Book (we gave the name a
penultimate stress) there was, on the shelf, a book called
How to Win Friends and Influence People, and there was also

the Bible in the multivolume Cassuto edition. Except that we didn't see the Book of Ezekiel.

We might tell how the clerks came and went and how we fell in love with several, but in fact only Mr. Twersky manned the store, and he would simply say, "What else" (with the words spaced out in rhythmic fashion).

At that time we'd think about Indulgences. That is, the writs of forgiveness that priests sold for money to sinners. Even though we hadn't committed any great sin (we'd stolen a cream puff from the kiosk and whatnot), we sought for ourselves a writ of forgiveness for all the sins we knew we'd commit in the future.

There's no need to point out (as we've already said in an earlier book) that the sun came and the sun went during those days as well.

[52]

Years before that Micah Raukher pushed us into a bougainvillea.

At the time, we hadn't yet heard of the man who was crucified at Golgotha, but without a doubt the number of thorns that pierced our flesh was greater by far than the number of nails that the Romans drove into him.

The kindergarten teacher took out the thorns with the help of a pair of tweezers, and we shed a tear like that boy in the picture that hung on the wall in every pediatric clinic in the country.

Micah Raukher stood in the corner and some thirty or forty years later died in a traffic accident. We were carried (which is to say, I was carried) by my grandfather, Isaac Emerich, in his heart, all the way to his house on Arlosoroff Street, next to the Monkey Park.

If the grandfather of the Crucified One (and not his Father in heaven) had taken him down from the cross, everything would have been different.

[53]

We've always wanted to know a man named Osip. We wanted to say Good morning, Osip—or Osip, what's up.

The name is suddenly cut off, but even afterward it sails on like a huge boat toward a place that had been prearranged.

It's unfortunate when a woman is named Griselda. On the whole, women should walk around without names.

We see them here and we see them there carrying a tragic basket or trying on a dress, and we can't forget for a moment how they're split within and become someone else.

In their childhood, which resembles a hoopoe bird (in gym shorts), and in their dotage as well (in shoes fitted to their feet in special stores), they are extremely beautiful.

[54]

This book is a book of moods. We could call it *The Book of Moods*.

Now we're filled with love, and now it's hatred. Sometimes we hate things we've loved or love things we've hated, and there is no end to it.

Once we hated spiders, and today we love them. Especially those with thin legs and round bodies. Because we don't drive them away (as others do), they spin webs in all sorts of places and come and go across the floor and along the walls, and sometimes they hang all night long over the bed, a pinky's length from our heads.

And when we sit at the table, intending to write, along comes a spider across the paper and it stands there over the words.

[55]

It's possible to leave the earth and watch it grow smaller and smaller. Till now we've seen this only in a dream.

Maybe the dead see such a sight. Or saints. In the commentary by Onkelos to the biblical passage about Abishag the Shunammite, it says that she lay beside the old king and sank into her thoughts. First (so it says) she drew the bedding out of herself. Then the king. Then the palace, and finally she hovered in a kind of spiritual space (as Onkelos puts it) in which there remained not a trace of anything material.

Most likely the elderly king looked at her and thought that his time too had come to pass away from this world and on to others, but memories seized him like crabs taking hold of a dead fish.

[56]

Now we're thinking about the woman psychoanalyst.

From the diploma on the wall we learned that she had made her way to people in the know in Switzerland. In our mind's eye we saw how she traveled there with her two breasts hidden within her suit jacket like stowaways.

Something about her recalls Glenn Gould. That chilly thing that makes us think of the hospital morgue in Cincinnati.

Picture an Orthodox Jew who has been exiled to the Canary Islands. He can't find a prayer shawl or phylacteries. There isn't any kosher food. He's looking for a synagogue. He wants to pray and chant his hymns, to whisper anguished petitions, but the people around him are selling watches.

[57]

A cow can hear the voice of the calf that's hers, even when hundreds of calves are mooing. She responds to his moo and he responds to hers.

Sometimes the movement of the heavenly bodies in their circuits is disturbed, and, for instance, the moon disappears, and then the cows lift their eyes to the sky and moo.

A question of considerable import is: Do weeds and trees experience longing? Once we saw an insurance agent weeping. He said something about a policy and suddenly burst into tears, and out of embarrassment we asked him only if he'd like some coffee.

He drank his coffee and wiped away the tears (people kept handkerchiefs in jacket pockets then) and stuffed the hanky into a pocket in his pants.

[58]

We also remember how the chorus teacher wept. He wept because the children threw chalk at one another and sent paper airplanes through the air and didn't listen when he shouted "Quiet!"

When a person who doesn't speak Hebrew hears the word *bakhah* (wept) he can't guess what it means. He might think that *bakhah* is a kind of tree used to build boats or a cookie (which is to say, a small flat cake).

Especially strange is that system of inflections by which we conjugate words like *bakhiti* (I wept), *bakhita* (you wept), *bakhah* (he wept), *bakhinu* (we wept), etcetera.

[59]

After her husband the Italian died, Mrs. Shtiasny lost her mind. She called Aunt Edith and my stepmother Francesca names like *krumme Ziege* (crooked goat) and *ein weiblicher Schnurrbart* (woman's mustache).

Once she woke Mr. Cohen, who was already a hundred and one, at midnight and asked him if it was A.M. now.

Within that madness she also understood things. She pointed to the corner of the room and said, "I'm not there," or she took the pictures off the wall in the hall while saying things like, "This is not a sun," or "These aren't horses."

[60]

In the end, Mrs. Shtiasny stopped speaking and only every once in a while would say, "*Die Unterwelt*" (that is, the Underworld).

(It's hard to say that Charles Darwin explained the world. The changing seasons. Day and night. The light that falls on an eel. The ends of words. A corridor.)

On a clear winter's day Mrs. Shtiasny sat in the yard. All the others went to eat and came back to their rooms for a nap. At three o'clock the hair on her head was lit by sunlight (the upper world) and burned with the colors of fire until dusk fell.

[61]

It's hard to believe that all this is taking place within a book. The people must be very small. Or maybe the power of imagination is employing signs (from among some twenty-plus) and turning them, by means of a kind of sorcery, into all these different things?

We've heard that people masturbate in front of the word *ishah* (woman). It's hard to see how the letters arouse them. Maybe the last one.

In the twelfth century a Chinese court calligrapher hanged himself from the palace rafters because he couldn't draw the character for *man* without thinking about what makes one.

It's highly probable that Jewish scribes copying sacred Jewish texts descend into the darkest of moods whenever they scribble a letter in error while writing a writ of divorce.

Once upon a time we knew a man whose name was Horovitz, and he'd always say, "Just one *v*."

[62]

When one goes astray, one really goes there. That is, one goes there as one goes home, and finds that being there has a shape and borders, and that people want to know what it's like between them. Being astray isn't easy, as the air is thin and the sky very high and the ground beneath one comes and goes.

Children also find their way there, but usually start crying until someone retrieves them. The elderly, on the other hand, don't look back. They don't remember other states. Some have even forgotten their names. But in the end they manage to find the toy elephant or the wooden train that once upon a time they'd misplaced.

[63]

Sometimes we start weeping for no reason at all, or for one we can barely recall.

Ezra Danischevsky's mother we saw just a single time. We were having soup she'd made and went out (Ezra and I) to play in the yard. Nonetheless, when we heard (thirty years later) that she'd died, tears welled up in us, even though we remembered only the *paff paff* sound that her slippers made.

Once we rushed a sick dog to the veterinarian's apartment. His name was Dr. Gottlieb and his apartment was on Clement Street. Because the door to his building was locked, we became extremely agitated and went around to the back of the building, where we saw a light and shouted the name of the street loudly.

[64]

We'd go down into the world of the dead if only we could meet William Saroyan. He would understand such things.
    In a certain respect we too are like Armenians exiled to California. Things like the names of department stores make us wonder.
    And also the news. Or the anchor's words: "First, the headlines." What seems right are the icebergs in the Arctic Circle or silent films, even when they're filled with war scenes.

Not that we don't fight for human rights, like Shulamit Aloni in the Knesset or that Communist woman whose name now escapes us.
    We do. And we don't forget for a single second the five fingers on our hand. There could, after all, be six or seven.

[65]

And we don't forget our shoes. Or the buttons on our sleeves. Or to breathe. This book treats all these things at all times, like a giant pair of bellows.

No one on the Left ever mentions Erzurum. Bless its residents. And the Yemenite villages (here and in Yemen). And the shopkeepers whom no one remembers, we remember.

And also Mr. Yaar, who sold shoes and because of some flaw deep in his throat made a tinny sound when he spoke. And the less-than-scrupulous taxi drivers. We haven't heard anyone mentioning them.

[66]

And the moon. On the Right they take it for granted, and on the Left they take it apart.

No one takes into account that it has no light of its own, and like the proletariat, depends on the graces of a larger light, one that's usually hidden.

And we always vote. Even when the polling station stinks of plucked chickens and seven or ten morose-looking poll workers are sitting at a long table.

We don't understand why all this is here (and isn't *not* here—which is to say, doesn't exist). None of the parties admit it. Let alone the particulars, like bobby pins and a thousand bras.

[67]

We salute the readers who've come this far. In the mean-time they and we (which is to say I) are walking on the earth's surface like circus bears balancing on a ball. Thousands of policemen walk like this (that is, like circus bears) and don't slip.

When we were little we thought about people in Australia and how their heads were upside down and yet they didn't fall.

The earth in fact comes from a dream (we think, like Aborigines) and returns to a dream. And if we sing (that is, speak) correctly, we return it to where it had been before the creation of the cosmos. Including flies, excrement, etcetera.

[68]

Once a poet came to visit and my first wife (here it's hard to speak in the plural) cooked a goose in his honor. We saw the poet's fingernails and his teeth and remembered the painting by Hieronymus Bosch of a fish eating a fish that was eating a fish.

Sometimes (in India or Africa) a leopard attacks a poet and this is part of the natural order, since all things in the end are swallowed by larger things, though we don't know who it is that swallows the world as a whole.

And so, one way or another, poems are written, and we too will now write a love poem to all the women reading this book:

A book you touch
Begins
Reading itself

[69]

Apropos love. In Ramat Gan (during the time of Mayor Krinitzi) a man named Kadoshkin walked from one end of Rav Kook Street, then the longest street in the country, to the other and back.

Kadoshkin held a cane in one hand and in the other he held a bottle. We don't know if the bottle was full or empty but if it was full it held water or vodka, because it was always transparent.

He'd stop before a display window, holding the bottle against his body (come to think of it, it held vodka) and call to the object behind the glass (he'd say "kettle," "shirt," "chair," etcetera).

During the winter the cane would become an umbrella, but the bottle remained a bottle. We believe that this man kept things in their proper place. And if he hadn't called them by name, they couldn't have maintained their form so precisely. And where would the Land of Israel be then?

[70]

We're wondering if the word *zarzif* (drizzle) is onomatopoeic. That is, a word that makes the sound the thing
makes. *Bakbook* (bottle), they say, does that.

Or *pkak* (cork). But not *lavlav* (pancreas). No one has
yet heard the sound that organ makes. But *parpar* (butter-
fly)—yes. People with a heightened sense of hearing can
hear this sound when butterflies flutter around them.

Mrs. Minoff, whom we've already mentioned (in chapter 13) spoke in onomatopoeia. She'd say, for instance, This
gluk gluk or *chin chin*, and sometimes only Francesca my
stepmother or Mrs. Shtiasny could follow her.

There were rumors that she'd slept with Mrs. Shtiasny's
Italian husband. But maybe she only slept next to him, and
in any event this has nothing to do with onomatopoeia.

[71]

We're trying to be humble, and modest. Even humor
seems like a sin today. And we should, so to speak, erase
ourselves so as to see only another. His birth. His childhood. His life.

We realize that these words don't amount to what's
usually called belles lettres. If there were a bank where
one could exchange literary currency for the currency
of life we'd go there and ask for the latter, even if it cost
us greatly.

And we'd go to the florist and buy a large bouquet of wildflowers for the woman who loves us (and pay for these with that currency) or stand in the kitchen where she usually stands and make lunch.

[72]

In December we're exiled to chillier regions and see death in action.

There my father (Andreas Avraham) hides from Francesca, my stepmother, records he bought because the money he receives (in transparent bills) isn't enough for her.

The music he listens to consists of a single sound, like the straight line on the monitor when the heart stops beating. The scent of eternity is like that of goulash. Everything's frozen over. Jokes one tells are revealed in full like that famous rainbow arched through a cloud. Each season extends to infinity. You stand there, and the streets run on beneath you. Women lie down forever. A faint soft sound like the fur of a foal (of a donkey) wafts through the air, and the colors are all pastel.

[73]

But sometimes the dead remain on the surface of the earth, like those we saw in Dublin, in the basement of St. Michan's Church.

There was a crusader there who died over six hundred years ago. He was large, and they sawed off his feet so he would fit into the coffin. And there was a thief who'd had his hands hacked off because he'd used them to steal, and his feet chopped off because he'd fled. And a nun who died at a ripe old age and whose tiny fingernails were preserved, as though she were still alive. And two brothers who rebelled against the British and were hanged, and their bodies, miraculously, didn't decompose at all until live Irishmen came and laid flowers at their heads and something wafting up from them (the flowers) made the men decompose.

Generally speaking. The world is full of miracles. How fingernails grow and hair gets long and we clip them both. How doors are slammed. And how the River Liffey, which cuts Dublin in two, runs on and on.

[74]

At times we're reminded of the future. How we'll sit by a window and see a mountain's silhouette. And we'll turn our head toward the room and see the silhouette of a man. We remember the scent of the morning papers during the twenties (of the twenty-first century).

We know this scrambling of time will cost us. We'll sink into a dark mood and, maybe, during the middle of the month see the moon when it's full. That great big pill of Prozac.

We've already talked of the woman psychoanalyst, but we haven't yet told our readers that once we saw a male analyst as well. Mostly we remember two things. The waiting room and that he was mortal.

If we could make a request of the readers we'd ask that they send us (c/o this book's publisher) all the words of the song that begins: "Five years passed for Mikha'el / While he danced away / He had no work he had to do / And he was free to play …"

[75]

That song broke our hearts and later so did Eleanor Rigby.

Here are some other things that break the heart: An old door. A glass left out in the yard. A woman's foot squeezed into shoes, so her toes become twisted. A grocer whose store no one goes into. Above all, a husband and wife who don't talk to each other. One-eyed cats. Junkyards. The stairwells of old buildings. A small boy on his way to school. Old women sitting all day by the window. Display windows with only a single item or two, coated with dust. A shopping list. Forty-watt bulbs. Signs with an ampersand (such as ZILBERSTEIN & CHAMNITZER), and when a person we love disappears (at a train station, for instance) into the distance.

[76]

Mrs. Shtiasny's Italian husband kept a bottle of brandy in the pantry and drank from it every so often.

One day during the fifties he opened the pantry door and a large package of noodles fell out and the noodles scattered across the floor.

This event resembled (in miniature) that meteor crashing into Siberia. We saw how thousands of trees were leveled at once in precisely the same formation as the noodles.

So it is that similar patterns run through the world. The lines in a leaf and the veins in the leg of a diabetic. The concave places in a woman's body and the valleys of regions like Provence. Heavenly bodies and uncut diamonds scattered about on a large table at the polishing workshop, and so on.

Mrs. Shtiasny got down on her knees and gathered up all the noodles, one by one. And because times were hard, she washed them under tap water and turned them into a soup.

[77]

And there was another thing. That a man knocked on the door and asked for a glass of water. He was carrying a large bundle of rugs on his shoulder and when he'd had enough to drink he spread one out on the hallway floor and said:

"This is authentic, from Paras" (he stressed the first sylla-ble, as Persian does).

The rug was the color of a pomegranate and held within it the forms of small birds and all sorts of flowers, and among them, equidistant from one another, were people.

He put down the glass on the edge of the rug and the small people near the glass got up from the rug and took a drink from the water left in the glass, then returned to their places among the birds and the flowers.

Many of the things recollected in this book are fiction. But the memory of this event, which we call (amongst ourselves) "the great thirst in the hall," is real.

[78]

Yesterday we read in the paper that a man broke a glass at his own wedding (in remembrance of the Temple's de-struction) and shards of glass went into the sole of his foot and he was taken directly from the chuppah to the hospital, and there they removed the glass from his flesh and bandaged his foot and as soon as he left he hired a lawyer and sued the owners of the banquet hall.

Imagine for a moment the crucified one coming down from the cross and hiring a lawyer. He'd have thrown his-tory off its course, and who knows what disasters might have ensued.

Better for a person to accept his fate and head off on his honeymoon while his foot is bleeding and only there, as the sheets turn red, let out a groan.

Sometimes things are sevenfold worse, as when a man manages to break the glass and his feet are fine but his wife then scowls for forty years.

[79]

Certain people are named Jorge and it's quite likely that they are scattered, not by chance but along the lines of geometric patterns (at the apex of a triangle or at a rectangle's corners), all across Israel.

And in fact it makes little difference if one Jorge takes the place of another. If he sometimes finds there an extra child or a refrigerator of a different color, he quickly gets used to it and to the woman who, in any event, everyone calls "Jorge's wife."

These are the turns life takes, and it takes us here and there, sometimes in Adidas sneakers and sometimes in Crocs and the like.

These changes are easier by night, when outlines blur, and nearly every man is willing to take in nearly every woman and vice versa.

[80]

And there are those who believe that movements like these (that is, who goes to whom, etc.) are scribbled in the stars, but we lift our eyes and see something else spelled out there.

First, what's written is written on infinite paper. Second, it's silent (that is, it can't be pronounced). And third, it's very very old.

But beneath that writing that no one can read we receive the great effulgence that's possible to see in tall towers of canned food.

At night, when the supermarket closes, the cashiers go out into the street and return to their room-and-a-half beneath what's written in the heavens—and no doubt it's written that death will surely come, and so we shouldn't worry so much. After all, we too are made of stardust, and there is no difference between the stuff of the stars and us.

[81]

Day after day Uncle Ladislaus lay in bed and wiggled his ears. And though he owned a donkey, he didn't make house calls. The donkey, which he tied to a pomegranate tree, brayed out of boredom and Aunt Matusya brought it leftover compote.

In those days you could see in the sky (there were no factories or street lights) a million stars. Below, between Herzl and Yahalom Streets, you sometimes saw the mayor, fat Krinitzi.

Our lives (which is to say, my life) was contained within a much smaller body, and all we wanted in this world was that this girl or that one would agree to be our girlfriend.

[82]

At this time most of the boys were named Tuvya. Girls were called Kinneret. The air was full of the scent of cypress trees (and countless lewd images). Teachers were usually called Yehudit.

But all this we've already said elsewhere. What good do those memories do? They're made of the stuff of dreams, and the stuff of dreams (as it says in the Talmud, Gittin 52) makes nothing happen.

We'll go with everyone to the mall and pass by the stores like herds of buffalo on the savanna. Then we'll sit in front of large plasma screen TVs.

After all, Uncle Ladislaus and Mrs. Shtiasny and her Italian husband and my stepmother Francesca are already dead. Others now are living.

And what's left of that world? Nothing. Only eternal truths, such as that two plus two equals four or that the sum of a triangle's angles is always one hundred and eighty.

[83]

Maybe we'll write (in a leaner style) a contemporary story. For instance:

At six o'clock, Zivit opened her eyes and yawned. She already heard the noise of the first bus from the street. I need to move to a new place, she thought to herself. Two cups stood on the table with coffee grounds in them. Only when her eyes fell on the cups did she remember Ohad. She turned her head toward the pillow beside her and saw his hairy back. She recognized the curl she'd made on his back before they fell asleep. Is this the man, she wondered, I'm destined to grow old with? Various thoughts passed through her mind. What about his son, she thought. Will Ohad want him to live with us? He's always saying that his ex is destroying the kid, and he almost went to a lawyer about it. And if it weren't for the social worker's report about the mother, the child would already be living with them. Am I cut out, she asked herself, to act as a mother to someone else's child? I doubt I can be a good mother to a child of my own.

She picked up her panties and bra from the rug and threw them into the hamper. Then she stood for a long while in front of the closet and finally chose a thong and a lace bra that was nearly see-through. She walked around in the room like that, wearing only her panties and bra, hoping that Ohad would open his eyes and see her, but he was fast asleep. No wonder, she thought, after last night's wild sex.

[84]

Some of our readers are no doubt saying to themselves: At last, a real story. I wonder what will happen next.

We don't know if we can say what will happen next. For that we'd need real inspiration, and inspiration, as we know, comes from somewhere else, like prophecy.

Where will Zivit go once she's fully dressed? Will she wake Ohad up before she leaves the apartment? And will Ohad go home, change his clothes, shower, and go from there to work? Will he call his ex and ask how the child is? Or maybe he'll call another woman? And so on and on with questions like these.

Once we met a woman named Rina Bartoldi. We remember that she said, "That hasn't yet been determined" (something to do with the age of the universe, 14.5 billion years or less). One could still see signs of beauty in her face, as in certain neighborhoods in south Tel Aviv.

We remember her even though some thirty years have passed because her age and the age of the universe were linked to one another, and because of the great distance between the two (that is, the two ages) and also because she stood in the world and spoke of its start and used the ugly word *determined*. All that and the fact that she looked like a pelican.

If this book didn't already have a name we'd call it *The Long Loneliness of Rina Bartoldi*.

[85]

Meanwhile (that is, between the first part of the previous section and the second) we also saw a doctor who specialized in hypertension.

The doctor himself was a little pale and his head tilted to the side. Generally speaking. There are many people whose head tilts to the side. Apparently it's hard to hold the head straight, and most of the time we're preoccupied with getting it right.

The doctor wasn't especially concerned about our blood pressure. We were there for all of seven minutes and still, as soon as we left we felt a kind of longing. We drove home through Kiryat Motzkin and Acre and Nahariya, and all the while the sun was on our left.

The moon hadn't yet risen, or maybe it was very pale and therefore we didn't see it. But we saw other things (the sea,

for instance, and the Nahariya train station) and all this we
thought we should share with our readers.

[86]

And also our dreams. That we're flying above a lake or
buying a kerosene stove with a chimney pipe for two hundred and twenty shekels.

We can also share with our readers that gray, amor-
phous primal sadness, which has no clear-cut place and
no particular reason for being, apart from the awful
apathy of things (like walls or entire cities or voices on
the radio) that take up their places, by themselves, while
nothing of them comes to us.

Once we saw the philosopher Yeshayahu Leibowitz in
Jerusalem, next to the old Bezalel Art Academy. He was
walking alone and carrying a jar in his hand.

[87]

We can do something godlike and create a person. Let's
call him Sha'ul Sachs. We'll give him a defect. One arm is
too long, or his chin is.

We'll lead him from place to place. He'll have a sun of his own and a moon. Others will call him Sha'ul, and some will call him Mr. Sachs.

He'll gradually grow older (or grow gradually older— we're entitled to choose between the two) and in the end he'll die and we can buy a rectangle in the newspaper— *Ma'ariv* or *Ha'aretz*—and write inside it: Sha'ul Sachs is no more.

The sun and the moon we'll leave in place. That way we can see the actual sun and the fictive one side by side, and the two moons.

Once, in Rome, next to the main train station, we went into a church and confessed before a priest.

This is what we said to him: Father, we've been carrying around heavy feelings of guilt. Heavy feelings of regret. Heavy feelings of hope. And, nonetheless, great love.

The priest said: Don't look in books. Sometimes they say one thing and God has decreed something else. We've heard that the red wine in Palestine is excellent.

[88]

In Alexandroupoli we met a Greek priest. He was sitting on a stool in front of a blacksmith's shop, holding a skewer in his hand and biting into the flesh of a grilled chicken.

We not live here, he said. On high mountain. Come each shix mont or sho, ate ... dreenk ... woamen ... haahaa.

He said something in Greek to the blacksmith and the blacksmith made a circle with his finger and thumb and stuck a finger of his other hand into the circle, maybe because he thought we hadn't understood the word *woamen*.

Beyond the shop there was a boulevard lined with palm trees and the Greek sun hovered on the horizon.

Then we went to the train station and there we were told that the train to Bulgaria would leave the following day at shix. The shky went red and the shun shet.

[89]

We've written elsewhere of our trip on the train to Bulgaria and how in the train there were only us and an old Bulgarian woman who drank wine and ate sugar and then what happened at the border crossing. Now we remember how we went to the city of Gabrovo because we'd heard it had a museum of humor.

It was a very hot day and maybe because of that no one in Gabrovo smiled when we asked where the museum was. In the museum (possibly in the entire city) there was what they call a blackout, and therefore the long neon lights weren't lit and the big ceiling fans were still. In most of the rooms there weren't any windows, and so we walked around in the dark, sweating profusely, and barely able to see the outlines (which is to say, the wooden frames) of the drawings. Moreover, in each room of the museum there stood a scowling Bulgarian woman in a guard's uniform.

We walked out into the light of day and saw, at the entrance to the museum, a gypsy making an old bear dance. We thought about all the memories that the bear must have held in its soul, and we were filled with awe.

[90]

Nothing comes to an end. There are extremely subtle things like a changing wind or passing thought and they are endless. Or things that are extremely thick like a cough or a clothes closet, and they too have no end. Or very slow things and very fast things that are fast and slow at once (like the memory of trains or mounds of coal) and therefore do not come to an end.

We saw physics textbooks and noticed how much sadness was trapped between the crumpled covers. We saw forks whose tines were taller than the spires of Notre Dame.

We saw things that were very large, like the space through which starlight passes, and we saw wonders such as a tree or a weather vane or a convoy of ants and Russian men and Belgian men (and women of course), and all of these things are endless.

[91]

Apropos Belgium. There was a thick-skinned woman selling latkes in the market in Antwerp. We asked for one
and she held the latke in her hand and didn't stretch her
hand out toward us. We stood there like that for a while,
as though in a film that had gotten stuck, until we realized
that first we had to offer up the coin and only then would
we receive the latke.

No doubt there were at the time latke thieves in Antwerp, and the woman was wary. And in fact the temptation to steal latkes in the Antwerp market is great.
Likewise the temptation to stick one's foot out (while
someone's walking blithely along) is great, in the market
at Antwerp, or elsewhere.

Or to slap someone without any reason. But no more
than that. Knives are foreign to our nature. Also pistols
and rifles.

But we're happy if soup gets spilled on someone, especially if it has chicken legs in it. Generally speaking. We're
happy at the sight of others' misfortune.

[92]

A journalist by the name of Kashkhanski wrote what he
wrote about another book of ours in which we spoke can-
didly of our lives.

He had a certain compassion about him, something one often finds in this country's builders. Most likely he had a hard time holding back tears, and would look as though through a fog at the white buildings of Tel Aviv.

The soft-mindedness of these people breaks our heart. Their feet are firmly planted in the wailing of Yosef Haim Brenner, but their spirits are free and they see what corresponds and doesn't, beginning with the *sefirah* Ayin (Nothing) and ending at the *sefirah* Malkhut (Kingdom)—which is to say, here. Where it says on the door, KASHKHANSKI.

Sometimes we miss those people, as the thrush longs for the dove. If we could meet them in the cafés of Tel Aviv, we would.

At night we toss from side to side and sometimes we dream that we're standing in a huge synagogue but instead of reading the prayer book everyone is reading the evening paper.

[93]

Our Great Pyrenees never has anything critical to say about us. He gets straight to the heart of things. If there's sorrow he sees sorrow. If it's joy—he sees the joy. Lesser dogs run away from him, and he doesn't even glance in their direction. The garbage-bin cats look on at him tranquilly and don't so much as budge from their places, not even if his fur almost grazes them as he passes.

His heart beats like the bell of a great temple, and in his eyes you can see the residue of the earliest stages of the universe (before the great break of creation).

And there is also a *person* like that. At a bakery. In the Arab village of Tarshiha. These are the ideas that Plato talked about. Dog. Man.

[94]

However you put it, the shards of things too are whole in their way. Once we met a book reviewer who wrote a sad poem.

No doubt she longed for a world without books or a world in which books contained just a single word, repeated endlessly.

It was clear that her room (most likely in a rented apartment) held a dirty glass shelf with four or five jars of face cream. And cassettes by that singer, what's her name? Mercedes Sosa.

And that same dress for whenever she went out, since the other dresses were cruel to her figure. And the books. Something about revolutions. And psychology. And Saramago's most recent novel.

We don't know if she shaved her legs, but if she did we'd suggest that she find an editor in chief, at a publishing house, who would stroke them.

[95]

This is also the answer to the Zen riddle about the sound of the one hand, and also the answer to the torments that Freud says a person endures. That is, that someone should touch someone, and so forth.

We think that our readers should use this book to look for another person. For instance, he should make it fall to the floor in a bar or a pub and then pick it up and ask a woman: Is this yours? Or put two glasses of red wine on it (we'll make sure it's big enough) or stick a knife into it and say, If the knife reaches the word *love*, you'll leave with me (we'll be sure to scatter the word throughout the book) or, If your back hurts you should put something hard under your head (and therefore we'll put out a hardback special edition).

Once (we remember) we used to pile books on a chair in order to reach high places.

[96]

We know a man who took one of the poet Shneor Zalman's books with him to his grave (which is to say, we *knew* him).

Our readers may not know this, but Shneor Zalman fought against Shmuel Yosef Agnon so that he, and not Agnon, might win the Swedish prize. Each of them (Shneor

Zalman and Agnon) had supporters, who sought to undermine one another and wrote letters and summoned ambassadors and convened mutually hostile committees.

Now both of these writers (and most of their readers) are dead and other writers (and readers) have taken their places, but we haven't heard of anyone (apart from that one man) taking a book with him to his grave.

At the cemetery we saw blank tombstones and we understood that most of these people were waiting for their spouses. But if you're going to take a book with you when you go, you should take Dale Carnegie's *How to Win Friends* ...

[97]

We don't know why happiness is so sad. Maybe because we see pieces of things, like a hand or a mezuzah, and want the whole thing.

My stepmother Francesca was already 83 and her eyes had gone dim. She could barely make out—and only then with great difficulty and with special lenses—very large shapes, and nonetheless she played bridge. She'd bring the cards very close to the lenses. At the same time she'd be speaking to Mrs. Shtiasny and Mrs. Minoff with great excitement about one thing or another.

What she didn't see she would feel, and what she couldn't feel she'd imagine, and she never said (or thought) that something was missing. If she'd gone up to the Himalayas the Rishis would have borne her aloft on their palms and burned incense at her feet.

What annoyed us was her habit of speaking only of practical matters. But this is one of our faults.

[98]

There are people who return the Divine Presence to Tel Aviv when they smoke cannabis. A great cloud wafts up over this city of sin, and all in a flash is forgiven.

People who are usually quite sharp (journalists, etcetera) find it a challenge to distinguish between a knife and fork, but a benevolent spirit enters their bones, and over the course of an hour or two they forget (which is so unlike them) all the appropriate ways of behaving.

We knew a man whose two names (first and last) were modern. Something like Yaron Yar-Ad, or Ran Ziv-Or (during the days of those kibbutz sandals that cost four hundred shekels). He was highly conscious politically, and therefore occasionally ate sashimi from the lunchtime menu. Now (under his cloud of hashish), he even loves settlers.

We need to check in Genesis to see on what day God created the grasses (just now it seems too hard to remember) and offer up a prayer of thanksgiving.

[99]

There are people in whose bodies cannabis can always be found, and they don't need to mix it with tobacco and light a cigarette, like that same distant relative (who was born in 1921) we used to call Uncle Shamu.

First, he jumped off an illegal immigrants' boat into the sea, near the coast of Caesarea, wearing a wide-brimmed hat.

Second, he immediately befriended (after two or three days) an Arab widow he'd met in Jaffa and went to live in her home. That widow in time became the only person who could speak high Hungarian in the entire Muslim world.

Third, he sold fountain pens, the nibs of which were made of gold. He found himself a small store on the border between Tel Aviv and Jaffa and over it hung the sign SHAMU PENS.

Fourth, he went into a mosque wrapped in a tallis.

But most of all, when he walked (from Tel Aviv to Jaffa and back) his shoes moved along at the height of the upper windows and the wide-brimmed hat on his head passed over the rooftops.

[100]

Generally speaking. What floats floats. There's nothing one can do about it. The news is divided into grammatical components. Syllables here, and consonants there. Sometimes you hear, as though it were Czech, a word with seventeen consonants.

Every woman opens her arms. White sheets flutter in the breeze. Suddenly Doctor Semmelweis arrives (he discovered the cause of childbed fever). You drink espresso and think about a cabbage salad. The Hebrew cantillation signs are homosexual. You go to the Home Center and ask for earphones and they give you birds. It seems to you that water is flowing under the streets. You see the rays of the sun one by one, as though in a child's drawing. No one is more lovable than the plumber. Yoel Hoffmann is the name of a powder. You hear the muezzin everywhere.

Evening is morning, although it's evening and the morning is morning, and nonetheless we don't get confused.

[101]

We haven't yet spoken of the great theories of mankind. Sometimes the spirit spins around itself like a whirlpool at sea, and the soul sinks.

Some people bow before nothing. Or plead to what's beyond the world to come and save them.

Whoever goes to hell goes to hell. Who's saved is saved. What do we know? Maybe far beyond the world, in a place unreached by the oldest starlight, a teddy bear sits and no one knows. Or a narcissus. Who doesn't get drunk on their scent?

We can now reveal to the readers of this book a deep secret, but they're not allowed to reveal it to readers of other books.

Feet follow one another. Hands cut through the air. The mouth opens and closes. The inner organs expand and contract, according to their nature. What's outside is standing or walking.

Prayers can be heard everywhere, whether a person says them aloud or not. Frogs need only themselves. The marsh reeds know the right direction.

And because these things are set forth here, it's a wonder this book is sold for so little.

[102]

Here we would like to introduce a new character. The landlord at 7 Nahalat Shivah Street, in Tel Aviv.

His name was given to him a day or two after he was born. They made meatballs and invited guests. The crystal dishes came out of the sideboard.

When he got bigger he rode on the tram, and at the Gymnasia he wore a hat with a visor. Now he's already old, and whenever he goes down a staircase he groans.

This is the man. His neighbor in the building next door (number 9) suits this chapter better. Readers can see (if they hide in the courtyard) how she goes down the stairs with the garbage. When she returns to her apartment she places different pots on the stove.

These two, granted, are minor characters, but they're major minor characters.

[103]

The words *falsification of corporate documents* frighten us. Maybe we're also committing such a crime. On the other hand, books like these can hardly be thought of as corporate documents, and we do our best not to lie. Witness the previous chapter.

Other writers lie all the time. They play around with names and change dates and whatnot. We, however, lied only with regard to the girls we had a crush on in fifth grade and sixth grade, because they're married now (though some are widows) and we've already seen how one of their husbands looked at us.

Writers should be brought to trial not over things like that but for inflicting boredom. There should be a clause about that in the criminal code. We, too, are sometimes guilty of this.

Imagine for a moment that we're found guilty of inflicting boredom on our readers and we're thrown into prison and sit there among the crime families. On second thought, that's better than sitting in Tel Aviv at fancy stores like the Bookworm.

[104]

Here we can relate the sly doings of Mrs. Shtiasny and her Italian husband and Mrs. Minoff and my stepmother Francesca, and how they traveled to the Rukenshtein Pension in the hills of Safed.

In those days no one traveled by taxi more than a few streets, and this only when something dire was involved. Nonetheless, they went by taxi, something that gave rise to considerable grumbling in the Austrian old age home. (They were accused of being haughty, wasting money, and the like.)

As a kind of punishment from on high (this is how the others saw it), Mrs. Shtiasny's Italian husband almost fell out of the taxi when he tried to slam the door while it was moving. To this day, some of the Arab elders of Acre remember the wondrous sight of a taxi passing through the Old City and the back door suddenly opening and a tall Jew being shot from it like a shell being fired from the barrel of a cannon and two women holding his legs and pulling him back inside.

At the Miron Junction Mrs. Minoff tried to slam the broken door and the whole thing happened again. That is, the door opened wide because of the wind and Mrs. Minoff tumbled out and was pulled back in by Mrs. Shtiasny and her Italian husband.

At the pension itself Mrs. Shtiasny's Italian husband suffered a bout of sleepwalking and wandering into Mrs. Minoff's room. But this we've already alluded to elsewhere.

[105]

From this incident with the taxi the readers can learn of the difference between fabrication (which we call fiction) and life.

In literature (which is to say, fabrication), the incident of the open taxi door would have occurred just once, as the author wanted only to refresh the readers' faith in the realism of the narrative. But in life? Life is full of great wonders, and things like this happen two or three times, much to the consternation and dismay of writers of a realist bent.

And another thing. A realist wouldn't have brought in my stepmother Francesca, since she wasn't really involved in these events. But in life? In life she sat beside the driver (whose name was Abramov) the entire trip, and the front doors of the taxi were fine. Details like these aren't mentioned in stories.

[106]

And another thing. We've heard about scholars of literature, but we haven't heard of scholars of life. Which is to say, people study one thing or another (like tissue or behavior). But life?

Scholars of literature, for instance, walk around within life. Maybe one needs to examine life from the perspective of those scholars. Once we knew a scholar who took medicine for various illnesses. We need to get to the root of all illnesses in order to understand life, and not to examine them one by one. Maybe there's a crack within them opening between the living soul and the crust that surrounds it.

Sometimes scholars of literature convene committees and there you can see flashes (like the flickering of the Northern Lights) of very sad things. A tie. Lipstick. Or the papers of the committee's agenda left behind in the hall after everyone has left.

[107]

To this day we don't understand why over the butcher shop in a Welsh village it says FAMILY BUTCHER. Maybe it refers to an ordinary store (that sells meat to housewives). In any event, we read the sign as though it was run by someone who slaughters families.

And apropos butchers. In Arab Nazareth we saw a sign in the window of a butcher shop on which it said WE SPEAK NORWEGIAN.

Signs like these lift our spirits. Like the names of banks in Portugal and Spain: BANCO ESPIRITO SANTO (which is to say, Bank of the Holy Spirit) or even the sign YOSEF AZRIEL ATTORNEY AT LAW AND NOTARY PUBLIC.

Once we saw, in Herzliya, beside the highway a big sign that said FUNN & CO.— REAL ESTATE BROKERS.

Generally speaking. The government should put signs on everything. They should put the sign HOUSE on every house and TREE on every tree and so on. This way we'd be better oriented. Maybe it should send a plane up into the sky to write out, in white smoke, the word WORLD.

[108]

We'd like to recommend Undencil. This is an excellent antifungal cream (for irritated skin). You can apply it between your toes or in the genital area and the itching vanishes instantly.

If readers have any advice to offer us about how to treat bladder irritation, we'd be grateful to them for that. They can write to us c/o the publisher or the township of Ma'alot, and the letters will be forwarded. We can also advise the readers how to lower their blood pressure by means of (the human) spirit (not the one that hovers over the face of the earth).

Generally speaking. Authors should display greater generosity toward their readers. But real generosity. Not like in certain places, where computers are stuffed with the dates of birthdays and spit out greetings on the right day.

We'd like to embrace all our readers. Men, women, the elderly, and children.

[109]

For what is man if not Uncle Shamu. Don't we all, in one way or another, wear a wide-brimmed hat and jump into the sea?

We should call all things by their first names. All dogs. All frogs. All trees. Once upon a time we took pity on a gourd that the gardener wanted to uproot, and so we called it Simcha.

How can it be that we walk around under the sky and nonetheless have an unconscious? Don't believe these lies. The world is large and wide and has no measure. And all is revealed.

[110]

One is greatly tempted to end the book with these words, but we need to be wary of too much truth.

We don't want to write (like the mystics) things that give off a whiff of sanctimony. We're trying to write a kind of train schedule.

Or an owner's manual. The sort of thing they distribute with appliances (like cell phones or pressure cookers), with instructions about how to operate them. Or something like the Kama Sutra.

True, all is revealed. But *how* is it revealed? It's revealed in the form of a certain woman, or another woman, and in all sorts of colors and all kinds of clothes and types of closets, and the whole thing is endless.

Once, at a country inn, in Ireland, we were waiting for breakfast to be brought out and no one came. After an hour or so we went to the kitchen and found the owner fast asleep on a chair with a bottle of whiskey before him on the table.

[111]

Elsewhere, on the east coast of England (in the town of Great Yarmouth), the owner of the bed and breakfast was overly attentive. She called her vacuum cleaner by its first name ("Henry") and put out seven kinds of cereal for breakfast.

We also remember the Hyatt Hotel in the Philippine city of Bangui. We were tended to there by women with names like Charity, Faith, and Honesty.

As for the rats at Hotel Long Spring, in Mekong (Taiwan), we've already written about them in another book (it's hard to believe that, in the entire history of world literature, the same rats have been mentioned in two different books).

This is the great diversity one finds in the world of hotels. Like a paint company's catalogue of colors.

[112]

We can't quite remember if we've already spoken about how Mr. Cohen from the Austrian old age home would raise a toast to the Emperor, Franz Josef.

Mr. Cohen was already a hundred, give or take, and was still sending letters of encouragement to the Emperor's son (or grandson). Every year on the Emperor's birthday he'd buy a bottle of champagne and go to my father's room and there they'd drink to him (that is, to the Emperor) or, more accurately, to his memory. My father wasn't a royalist, but he did like his liquor.

We, on the other hand, are of the opinion, like Mr. Cohen, that the monarchy should be restored. Not only in Austria. Everywhere.

And that the words of the prayer Avinu Malkeinu (Our Father Our King) should be offered up in both directions. And though the prayer is cast in the masculine form, we'd rather see women reign in both places (in heaven, that is, and on earth).

[113]

My father Andreas liked to play tricks on people. Mostly on his sister, my Aunt Edith.

Every year, on April 1, he'd come up with another prank. Once he started muttering strange syllables and wrote a note to my aunt saying that he had vowed from that day on to speak only Mandarin. Another time he borrowed a tallis and prayer book from the gardener at the old age home, and when my Aunt Edith came to his room he wrapped himself in the tallis and called out in a loud voice and mimicked the chanting of the cantor and the prayers. My Aunt Edith was as innocent as a flock of lambs and it never occurred to her that her brother was playing a trick on her.

Sometimes we too (which is to say, I) thought that he'd lost his mind, like the time that he tossed a thin book into the air, as though he were throwing a boomerang, and shouted "Balthazar." We had no idea who Balthazar was but since my father repeated this act some twenty times or more we remember the name to this day.

When he was serious, he was too serious. But that's already another story.

[114]

We're asking ourselves what the point of this book is or of books in general.

We've never seen books classified by genre. That is, we've seen them classified, but not correctly. What's the point of classifying books as fiction or contemplative literature, for instance, when fiction is part and parcel of contemplation and contemplation is entirely a matter of fiction?

Or take, for instance, science books. These aren't stories? Accurate ones. But stories nonetheless. Or the distinction between biographies and novels. Is there a biography that isn't a novel? Or a novel that isn't the story of a life?

If books are going to be classified by genre, it should be done in an entirely different manner. First, one has to distinguish between happy books and sad books. Not books that make one happy or make one sad. Happy books, plain and simple. A book that can laugh or smile or cry. The book itself. The reader can behave however he likes.

Critics, for example, cry at the sight of happy books and are happy in the face of books that cry. The marble-like faces of academicians are summoned before books of every sort. No wonder most of them (that is, most of the books) get offended.

Apart from the classification by feelings, it's also possible to classify books by subject matter. The principal group here would be books about pelicans. Or a large group of books about shoreline rock formations. Here too there are secondary classifications (such as pelicans according to their coloration or shore formations according to their shape, and so forth). But better to classify them (that is, the books) by their feelings.

[115]

At first glance this book would seem to be a hybrid. That is, a book that sometimes laughs and sometimes cries. But in fact (as the logicians say), it's laughing and crying at once, and to the same degree.

The protagonist of this book is the human being. God is a minor character. And so it (that is, the book) is a total failure, since it never really gets to the heart of one or the other. If it were printed on thinner paper we'd suggest the reader use it for rolling cigarettes. The smoke would write the book in the air as it really is.

My father (Avraham Andreas) knew how to blow smoke rings. Much to our amazement he could smoke an entire cigarette without it falling apart. That is, the whole thing would turn into one long tube of ash, and he wouldn't have to tap it—not even once—on the ashtray.

[116]

When we took him (that is, my father) by taxi for an x-ray, a pickup truck drove in front of us and a large Doberman sat in the back of the vehicle.

Throughout the trip the dog was looking at my father and my father looked at the dog until we got to the hospital. There they told us that a large spot had been found on my father's abdomen (he was already 86), but, out of courtesy, they didn't mention the word cancer.

On the way back to the old age home the same pickup truck was driving ahead of us (we recognized the license plate number) but the dog was no longer there. When we got to his room, my father put one string quintet or another on the record player, poured himself a glass of cognac, and said: You don't need to tell me. I know. It's over.

[117]

At night we hear the jackals and the moon is twice as large. Wild boars come up to the fence and dogs bark. We see the silhouette of the mountain over the house. The mountain itself is black.

This is the Philharmonic of the Galilee's Hills. Immigrants from Morocco and Russia, the Druze and the Christians and the Muslims, all have subscriptions to this orchestra.

Citizens of Tel Aviv sit, shut in a hall, in rows, their backs straight, and listen to their own concert. All is finely crafted. Movement by movement. The musicians come in at just the right time. The conductor waves his hands like one of those miserable souls afflicted with an obsession for order and cleanliness. The Galileans, on the other hand, lie down, each in his bed, on the enormous stage of a much greater concert.

At midnight the last of the jackals falls silent. The wild boars return to the thickets, and the dogs go into their doghouses. Each one dreams. The jackal dreams. The boar dreams. The dogs dream, and the human beings dream as well. If the children's books are to be believed, so do the moon and the mountain.

[118]

Around three o'clock in the morning all sorts of things come to mind. That we said something stupid. That we were spoken to coarsely. That people we've loved have died and people we love are far away. That we're old now. That everything's gradually slipping away.

In the night air we see loose women. Killing fields. Natural disasters. Jackals are howling outside again, and the dog is barking. Things that were—won't return.

There's shouting everywhere. Houses on fire. Thoughts are burning. There's an air of depression, like a cold front, moving in from the west. We're walking barefoot along bookshelves that serve no purpose, turned in as they are on themselves, and ponderous, like geological formations in a canyon's walls. Whence cometh my help, we think. And take a Valium.

[119]

Someone said, "Get hold of yourself." We've always wanted to get hold of ourselves, but to do this we'd need to extend our arms considerably, and how could we stand on the ground if we were in fact to get hold of ourselves (feet and all).

Imagine that we could cradle ourselves like that and move from place to place like large babies carrying themselves. We'd calm ourselves down like mothers do when they rock their babies in the air and sing them lullabies.

People would come with claims only against themselves and with the soles of their feet laid bare. Maybe they'd even be carrying themselves (getting hold of themselves) while they're naked. So nothing would be concealed from them, and they'd see themselves completely, as a mother sees her baby while she's changing a diaper.

True. We'd no longer be counted among the bipeds. Our legs might atrophy. Crows would undoubtedly gaze at us in amazement. Maybe we'd be defined in dictionaries as a kind of clumsy bird (lacking wings and feathers) that hovers heavily as it carries itself over the face of the earth. But we wouldn't be wanting.

[120]

The sun sets in any event, even if you try hypnosis to get it to stop in the sky.

You can sit in Nahariya by the sea and see for yourself. Like we did once, when we met with the editor in chief at Café Kapulski.

The editor in chief didn't know, of course, that we were trying to do this, and so we could focus on the hypnosis only when he turned to eat his tuna sandwich or took documents out of his briefcase. Maybe that's why it wouldn't work. That is, because we weren't able to look at the sun the entire time as it was setting.

We've not yet revealed to a soul that we have hidden powers. We can, for example, break a thought in two and join an entirely new thought to one of the broken halves. Or we can move our hand.

You can go to Café Kapulski in Nahariya and try these things. You might have some luck, even with the sun.

[121]

Among our powers is the power to draw women toward us.

We've been endowed with this only to a moderate extent. At times a women would walk toward us as though against her will, but usually this was a woman we weren't interested in, like women whose names were Kinneret Lipshitz or Zahara. We were drawn to darker women, but more often than not they would march on, in a straight line (without, that is, veering off in our direction).

Nevertheless we lift up a prayer of thanksgiving for every woman who showed us kindness. One shouldn't take these things lightly. That, and the green carpet that covers the hills during the rainy season. Or the migration of storks. Or the laundry lines with their white sheets on the rooftops. Or the train's whistle or the boat's horn as it comes into port. Or the perfume wafting in the theater lobby. All are blessings from God that exert an influence over us. And, especially, the gentle swish of dresses as women take them off.

[122]

We saw a beautiful woman during the Days of Awe. She glanced from behind the screen of the women's section like a half moon revealed through a cloud.

With the blowing of the shofar our hearts were split in two and we fell in love with her. The prayer books and holy ark swirled in the space of the synagogue, like in a painting by Chagall. Every so often the screen was shifted and her face would appear then vanish. Lines from hymns were scattered, like Lego pieces, in the air.

Finally we couldn't stand the screen any longer and went up to the edge of the women's section and stared toward the swarm of kerchiefs that moved like a field of wheat in the wind. We didn't see her, and nonetheless union with her was brought about, facing away, so that the world would go on. Otherwise, it would have returned to the darkness that preceded the chaos and void, and the voice.

In a certain sense one might say that at that moment we created the doors and frames through which people pass, and the vast range of possibilities within the kaleidoscope we call life.

[123]

Yesterday we came home and wanted to die. But then we remembered the laundry marks that are put on clothes (the letter *nun* for Nahman and for Shalom Nehemkin also a *nun*, though a *shin* would have been more appropriate) and our spirits revived.

There's great vitality in laundry marks and in people who put them on each article of clothing. And later, at a large laundry, clothes are sorted by these marks and returned, clean and pressed, to their owners.

These are the things that require our attention in a novel. So that the clothes of the main character won't get mixed up with those of the minor ones. Especially in a serious novel. Imagine what would happen if, in the middle of the action (when critical things were taking place), the main character was running around with a shirt three sizes too small for him. No one would take the book seriously.

Or picture a novel in which a man walks around in a woman's clothes and a woman is wearing the clothes of a man. On second thought, such a thing is entirely plausible (and even called for) in a novel where all the main characters are transvestites. But these sorts of novels are quite rare, and as a rule it's wise not to mix up the clothes.

[124]

Today is Christmas. We're thinking about virgin births. Unlike that Portuguese writer, Saramago, we believe in the sanctity of that moment. There wasn't an infant in the world, and suddenly there was.

And we too are the product of a virgin birth. We were born twice. First when a woman of flesh and blood delivered us in the ordinary manner. Later, like everyone, we were wiped off the face of the earth with the people who were sent to the ovens. And if we're alive, we are—like some sad kind of miracle—among the babies now in the ground, or far above in the place where the smoke from the chimneys ascended. Beyond history.

[125]

The counting did in fact begin, as the Christians have it, with the birth of the infant Jesus. But it concluded with the birth of Adolf. We were given just 1,889 years of life.

Now we're in the age of ash. Beyond time. As though in a game that has come to an end. There's no more movement on the field. Just kicks toward the goal. Everything only *seems* to be. A thin wash of color covers it all, and beneath that—blackness.

Only giraffes remain. Mountains. Wisps of clouds. Celestial bodies. Woods. Bodies of water and shells of men. Europe, apparently. Hallucinations. A real sun rises over nothing.

[126]

We know that we need to say something amusing now. Some sort of joke. Or an anecdote. Something about a great love.

How, in spite of everything, the world renews itself. Phone books, for instance. Countless men and women brought together, and one could call them all.

We remember how, when we were little, maybe in sixth grade, we'd flip through the phone book and look for funny names. We found the name Dr. Ochs and called the number and when a man answered Yes (with a German accent) we said: Moooo ...

Which is how every ox finds its mate. And the male chiropractor a female chiropractor. A male accountant a woman who also manages accounts.

We remember how, in those days, we'd visit each other on Raleigh bikes (with a bell) and ride together to the river. Girls with names like Tzila would shake their heads and their braids would fly in the air. The soles of the teachers' feet would sweat, because they were wearing leather shoes even during the summer (they'd come from the Holocaust), and if there were empty places they'd be filled up at once with oranges and tangerines.

[127]

Everyone came for a brief while and went with joy to his death.

And how did they die? One way or another. Shamaya Davidson, for instance, who was an English teacher, tried to hurdle a low barrier. Just two rows of cinder blocks. He completed the first part of the jump, which is to say, up to the point where the body begins to return to the ground. But instead of landing, he kept on rising through the air.

There was also a Hebrew teacher. He was walking down the hall and suddenly died of happiness. We've heard that in the old farming cooperatives people would slip between two heavy books, as though they were flowers, and press themselves dry. In Tel Aviv, people would lie (when they felt the moment was nigh) down beneath a café table, and the waiter would put a piece of cream cake on their belly.

And there were people like my grandfather, Isaac Emerich, who took off their clothes and got into bed, and thus, quietly, slept while they were dying.

[128]

We're extremely proud of the previous chapter. It's a shame we can't show it to our dead relatives.

Then again, we could go to a specialist who calls the dead back to this world and speaks with them. We knew a man like that once, but he died, and now we need someone to bring him back as well. Maybe we should look in the yellow pages, under the listing "Spiritual Practice."

Imagine that we're trying to bring Aunt Edith back, and by mistake we summon Attila the Hun. Or Ben Gurion. What would we say? Sorry to disturb you? Better to let them be and wait until we ourselves go to them.

On the other hand, it's possible that we're already dead and that the world we see around us is in fact the world to come, and the government bureaus and the government itself are a kind of photographic negative of the previous world, but we just don't know it.

Once we knew a woman who was always saying, "Oy, I'm dying." Maybe she knew more than it seemed.

[129]

This might be the last book that we'll write. I wonder how it will end. What its final words will be. Joyce, for example, finished his final book with the word *the*.

We've always thought it extremely strange that movies (and books) end with the word *End*. Moreover, sometimes the definite article's added.

Maybe we'll end with another word altogether. We'll do what we did when we were little. We'll shut our eyes and open the dictionary (or some other book) and put our finger on one of the pages and the word that our finger lands on will be the last one.

Imagine if the word turns out to be *prow*. Or *Binyamina*. Or *epaulettes*. Or *hydraulic*. Or *gurgle* (which is probably onomatopoeic). Or *drowse*. Or *you*.

[130]

We could, toward the end of the book, tell about a murder, and then when the woman asks, Who killed him, the detective will answer, *You*.

Or we could make it a love story, and the woman will ask, And who is that woman you always dream of, and the man will answer, *You*.

And what then? What happens in books after they end? Then, and only then, does the true story begin. Again there's no end. No division between different things. All the colors come at once. Forms are found within each other, even if that involves a contradiction (a square circle, for instance, etcetera). Scents mix. There's a spectrum of sounds that Maria Callas never even dreamt of. The size of the pages (after the last one) is infinite. They're white like the Siberian tundra in winter. Whoever reads those pages reads himself to death.

[131]

Saroyan understood these things. He'd always fall toward those other pages and return (out of compassion) to the book itself. He knew the old women who sifted lentils, and the Mexican workers' dogs.

There was never a more religious man, and therefore he drank and gambled and went to whorehouses (in books and beyond them), and every word he wrote was charged, like high tension power lines, with thousands of volts.

And he was a great thief. If we're missing a key we can be sure it's in the celestial pocket of his suit. He'd lift the mustache right off our face, and even slip our wife away.

In fact we've forgotten our name and think we're called Saroyan. When someone says Yoel Hoffmann, we think he's speaking to another person.

No wonder it's so hard to separate Siamese twins. Because they have just a single heart, one of them usually dies.

Today the muses, damn them, went elsewhere. They come and go as they like, and we're in their hands like a weather vane in the wind.

We haven't seen them with our actual eyes, but it's said that there are seven. And in fact, when they all come at once, the noise is unbearable. One says Write this, and another Write that, and they fight with each other and sometimes coax us into writing drivel, or worse, what's true.

Mostly they sing like a choir of angels or those women in Hawaii who hang leis from their necks and sway their hips. But when an evil spirit gets into them, each one goes into a corner of the room and screams. And then you sink into the lowest of spirits and begin to write—like some kind of clerk—all sorts of facts. And she left. And the phone rang. And the train arrived at the station. And the street was wet with rain. And they drew pistols, etcetera etcetera.

These are the muses of sanity, destroyers of art—who tempt writers and poets to enter into a marriage with them, then send them to take out the garbage, or fix the faucet.

Dzhokhar Akhmadov, a poet from Chechnya, said to us once: You see eagles whose wingspan covers Grozny and all the surrounding plains. My elderly mother looks out through the window, but the glass is broken. Nights crawl like a hungry hyena. You've come from a far-off place and so my soul grows faint. Have you ever seen a Muslim cloud? Or a cloud that's Greek Orthodox?

People died of tuberculosis. Some in stairwells, with fire from the bombs lighting up their faces. I didn't know you before today, but I've long known you would come, and now we can go to a single grave. You see these hands? Think of an infant and think of a mortar.

[134]

As though in a slaughterhouse, we need to strip off all of our skin—down to the very last piece. We're the butcher and also the beast. And if the blood doesn't flow toward the drainage channels, there is no literature and there is no poetry.

Once we sat in a Tel Aviv café (we realize there's more to Tel Aviv than cafés, but when we go there we've nowhere to sleep), and we saw through the glass a woman pushing a carriage and in the carriage there was a baby. Where is that woman now? And the baby?

Poetry's found in the melting tar of summer rooftops, in which you can see the imprint of the soles of shoes.

We remember that Uncle Shamu once held a fountain pen up to the sun and with his other hand pointed to the nib and said: See, it's gold.

Since we've thought of Uncle Shamu we've also thought of Dr. Kalish, who'd say the words "as well" (*und auch*) for no reason at all.

Dr. Kalish was a doctor of the humanities. He'd studied ancient history, or something like it, at the University of Leipzig and came to Palestine with Dr. Zoltan Forschner (who was a medical doctor), my Aunt Edith's husband.

Why are we mentioning all these things? Because when the Italians bombed Tel Aviv (during the second world war) Dr. Kalish's house was cut in two and Dr. Kalish and his wife (Frau Dr. Kalish) were exposed to the world as they were sitting at the kitchen table and eating an omelet.

During that same bombardment many people died, but Dr. Kalish and his wife were brought down on a ladder from the third floor, and from there they took a taxi to my Aunt Edith and her husband Zoltan, and they stayed with them (in their other room) for something like half a year.

We were six or seven then, and now can confess that we'd go to my Aunt Edith's apartment (five buildings away) only to hear Dr. Kalish say *und auch* (as well).

He'd say, for instance, "Where is the skillet *und auch*," or "What time is it *und auch*," or "The Germans are retreating *und auch*," or "Emma"—this was Frau Dr. Kalish's name— "come here please *und auch*," and so on.

For days (no, weeks and months) we'd think about what this *und auch* meant. That is, we realized that Dr. Kalish saw much more than other people did, but we didn't know what he saw.

Once we plucked up our courage and we too said *und auch* (something along the lines of "What does it say in this book *und auch*"), but Dr. Kalish just looked at us, surprised.

Today we think it should be mandatory, by law, for all people to use this expression at the end of every sentence. So as not to get too smug.

[137]

There's someone else we wanted to talk about but we've forgotten his name and how he looks.

We remember only the other things. That he was a body's length from the earth's surface. That he came near and grew distant. That night came over him and the day made him bright, and things of this sort.

We can't recall anyone more precisely. Therefore we miss him, and because we can't remember his name, our longing is greater than we can say.

This person is with us wherever we go, and without him we'd die of a broken heart. And if this seems overly clever to someone, then maybe he should look at himself.

This man is also the hero of this book that we're writing (and of all the books that we've written to date). If we could bring him to mind, we wouldn't need to write.

[138]

We've already discussed Japan in this book. Here we simply want to mention the two distinguished prostitutes from Kyoto.

The first bowed deeply and said: We welcome you under our meager roof. We're honored that you've chosen this lowly establishment. With the greatest possible humility we would like to begin by playing the samisen for you, and to the sound of its music a *maiko* (young geisha), who goes by the name of Rose's Scent, will dance before you an ancient dance of desire. Ten thousand yen.

The second bowed more deeply still and said: Of late the autumn wind has blown, and the maple leaves are turning red. Within our humble rooms you can meet Cherry Blossom, who is, it's true, thirty-six, but full of tricks, or Drawn Sword, who can bend herself, for your distinguished pleasure, in all four directions. Twenty thousand yen. And Lotus Flower, about whom you've no doubt heard, is thirty.

Cherry Blossom took off her obi but didn't remove her kimono. She bowed deeply and said: Mr. Gaijin (Mister Foreign Man). Does Japan please you? Have you seen the rock garden at Ryoanji? Or the great statue of the Buddha at Nara? Does Mr. Gaijin know that it's possible to crawl through his nostrils?

Yes. Cherry Blossom lives in Kyoto. Cherry Blossom's mother was also a geisha. Cherry Blossom's younger sister is a *maiko* at the House of the Full Moon, in the Gion Quarter.

Has Mr. Gaijin left a wife behind in his country? Is her hair blonde? Cherry Blossom is no longer young, but is her figure not that of a young woman?

Then Cherry Blossom took up the koto and plucked on its strings the ancient song,

> A moon in the pond—
> But the waters do not break,
> And the moon stays dry.

Sometimes the waters of the pond are stirred and the moon disappears. Then we go out to the street at four thirty in the morning and see the silhouette of the newspaper deliveryman and hear the paper hitting the pavement. The air is very cold at this hour and even one's memories freeze. Women we've known are suspended in inner space like icicles.

At five thirty the municipality turns off the streetlights and at six the sun, the Sonne (that son of a bitch), does what it does behind the post office. In the street, the garbage truck moves along then stops. We greet Beber, the garbageman, and at that very moment the sun comes up, glorious and dripping with sex, over the roof of the post office, and so we stand there, two men and one large woman, till the driver of the garbage truck yells out, Nu, Beber, let's go already.

[141]

We owe nothing to no one. Certainly not a story. If we'd like we could write a single word 7,837 times. A word is as cheap as a stick. Or we could compose our sentences along the lines of Japanese syntax (that is, from the end to the beginning). Or insist that the publisher burn the bottom edge of the book so that the reader's hand will be blackened by the charcoaled page.

Whoever doesn't get it can go to hell. Let all those intellectuals with their pursed lips go to hell and take their stash of Paxil with them. The women too. Things would be better between us without all that wisdom of *I'm look-ing for myself*, and so forth.

We suggest that you put your hand behind the book-shelves and knock the books over onto the floor. You can see how they open in the air like a fan.

And you're entitled to smash all the light bulbs. Why not. You'll see the children glow with joy. You'll tell them that now it's time for the other lights.

[142]

There's a certain amount of noise in Mrs. Rauschenberg's name. But she was without a doubt the quietest woman we've ever known.

Like Sisera's mother, she sat all day by the window and looked out toward the villages of Hiriyya and Sakiyya (which were there before the '48 war).

No one knew what Mrs. Rauschenberg was thinking. If this were a story we'd write that she'd lost such and such at Auschwitz. But in fact it wasn't possible to know if she'd ever had anything to lose.

That's all. If we had any other information (we could, for instance, write that we remember the scent of Yardley soap that wafted up from her, or the fine netting that cov-

ered the hair on her head), we wouldn't hide this from
our readers.

[143]

We think that Mrs. Rauschenberg was silent till the day
she died, and Miss Rigby (from the Beatles' song) also
didn't speak very often.

Because what, at this point, is there to say? At most one
has to tell the grocer what one wants, or else one gets a
mango instead of tomatoes.

We were at the university and saw that people go into
rooms at regular intervals and one person then speaks
before them for a very long time. We remember things of
that sort from our childhood, when we heard the croak-
ing of frogs or when the cicadas (in Japan, for example)
sent up their sound day and night, during the summer.

But the frogs and cicadas say just one thing, which is
most likely very important. Something about the water in
the swamp, or the warm air, or the desperate need to mate.

And that's how it should be in the university. A person
should enter and say to everyone (even for an hour and
a half or more) things like "I'm Mattityahu. My mother's
name is Rivkah. My father is Eliezar. Yes, please ..." And
so on.

[144]

Because once we traveled by bus from Tiberias to Tel Aviv
and beside us sat a woman who had a large basket of eggs
on her lap.

We didn't speak at all, but by the time we reached the
town of Tabor a great closeness had developed between
us and at Hadera we could no longer (which is to say, I
could no longer) think of ourselves as alone in the world.

The hardest moment came at the Central Bus Station
when the woman got off the bus and went somewhere
else. Then we thought (as our heart emptied), What's Iphi-
genia in Aulis to us? Or macroeconomics? Or sociology?
Or the conjugation of verbs? Or theories concerning me-
tallic strength and tensility? Or generally, what's what they
call perspective or point of view to us? We wanted to lie
down under the great wheels of the bus and die. And we
swear before man and eternity (and that includes all the
psychologists and their ilk) that we've never been more
sane than we were at that moment, when that woman
with the eggs left us behind.

[145]

Each time we think that we've come to the end of the
book we're reminded of something else to say. We remember how our children were very young and how, as

we held their hands and hurried from place to place, they flew in the wind like kites.

We also recall how we were offended in all sorts of places. Especially in Switzerland. Everything there (including the landscape) was so utterly orderly, and as a result we were hurt to the core (or maybe that should be to the cores).

The visible police directed things outside, and the hidden police held sway within. The moment we crossed the border, we were sent (one can't say we were thrown, since no one throws things there) into an internal prison, one of those places where everyone sits in a cell made of iron and sees his neighbors through bars on the side and his guards through bars in front of him.

We also recall Lake Biwa, which resembles a huge violin, and when it's still one can see the cities on the opposite shore doubled there, above and in the water.

[146]

And we remember also the thousands of candles that the Japanese float on the surface of the lake. These are the souls of family ancestors and maybe my great-grandfather Ausiás Goldschlag was among them as well.

We're imagining him hovering over the face of the waters, his great beard singed by the flame of the candle and the Japanese all around him staring in wonder but bowing politely.

One should perhaps explain these memories (a brain and so on) but we're sparing our readers explanations of that sort. For they too (the readers) deserve a little rest. So they can spread the fields of their recollection far from the skull and toward the cities and the villages of Europe, toward Baghdad and Kurdistan and Morocco and Algeria, enormous regions—larger than the box of the brain by a factor of more than a million.

In the end, the paper boats sink in the water and the candles descend to the bottom of the lake. The celebrants shake the dust from their kimonos and go home. And this too we won't let anyone explain.

[147]

Once, in Mea She'arim, we ran into a demonstration against the practice of carrying out autopsies. Garbage bins were burning in all four corners of Sabbath Square. People shouting verses from the Psalms were shoving us up the slope on Strauss Street. The smoke from the burning plastic brought tears to our eyes and for a moment we imagined that we were weeping for the dead whose dignity had been violated.

In fact, we thought (like a wandering violinist who stumbles onto a string orchestra)—Why do we need to cut into the flesh of someone after they die? Finally, after a life of sorrow and trouble a man lies in absolute peace on his back. If one really wants to know what the cause of death is one could write on the relevant documents "Birth," and if one really wants to know what the cause of birth is, one could write there "Death." And even if we cut into the dead man's tissue we'll find more tissue beneath it and beneath that still more, whereas the secret is much more likely to be found in the open mouth of the dead man, out of which his spirit passed, or in the open mouth of the world, proof of which lies in the sun and stars.

[148]

We're asking ourselves if, before the creation of the world, it was determined that the great novels (*War and Peace* or *Crime and Punishment*) would be written.

It's clear that God didn't conceive of them. He's very sparing with words, and when he does speak the results are seismic (see for instance Genesis 1), but it may well be that these works were, as they say, within him, like civilization as a whole.

Sometimes writers say that they're only vessels in the hands of God. Some French writers have even tried what's called automatic writing. That is, they themselves didn't interfere in what was written on the paper. One of them would write the word *shutters* maybe seventy times. Most likely at that very moment God felt a terrible sense of constriction.

My grandfather, Isaac Emerich, would sigh every so often and say, *Ach, mein lieber gott* (Oh, Good Lord), but if we ask ourselves if his complaint was predetermined as well, we'll never find our way out of this maze, not even if we address the question to the Department of Philosophy, in writing.

[149]

Tonight is New Year's Eve. Tomorrow's January 1, 2009. We greet our readers (also those who don't read our books) and wish them this: that in the coming year they should read only good books. Michael Rips's *The Face of a Naked Lady*, for instance.

There's no point in talking about wretched humanity that's sending artillery shells in every direction tonight. God have mercy on everyone.

[150]

Now it's below zero. Think about these words *below zero*. Less than nothing.

When we were in Japan we read in books by religious sages that it's possible to get below zero and then to walk around above zero as though one were still beneath it. Something like abstracting the form from things and nevertheless leaving them as they are.

Once we knew a woman by the name of Rivkah who always said "It's nothing," and nevertheless bought herself blouses and dresses and the like.

As far as we're concerned, we prefer the rabbis
    a) because of their beards
    b) because of their Yiddish
    c) because they know that everything's nothing but
    don't say so, so as not to spread sorrow through the
    world.

[151]

Outside, everything's frozen. We bring the dogs into the house. The cats go into the empty doghouses and warm themselves against each other's bodies. But what do the wild boars in the brush do? The jackals? The birds?

Language too gets twisted. Entire words freeze in the mouth, and we need to stand beside the stove to thaw them out.

Which reminds us of the story that Wilhelm Busch wrote about Peter, who wouldn't heed the warnings he'd received and went out to play one winter's day and didn't return. His father and mother sat at home and wept, but a hunter found him in the woods and brought him back, frozen as a block of ice, and his father and mother were very happy and led him toward the stove and watched with joy as he thawed out, but, alas, in the end, all that remained of him was a puddle of water and his broken-hearted parents gathered the water up into a jar and put it on the shelf between a jar labeled CUCUMBERS and another labeled SALT and wrote on it PETER.

[152]

We forgot to wish the psychologists a Happy New Year. No doubt the cold makes it harder for them to look into souls.

If only the New Year would bring about a condition in which their souls would melt (as one melts lead) into the great form of the soul of the world, and there'd no longer be any separation between their eyes (behind glasses) and the eyes of the people they're looking into. And that the rule against hugging others might be dropped, and, above all, that someone would hug them.

Because there is no loneliness greater than that of the psychologist. His thought is always doubled, as he's forced to consider thought upon thought, and sometimes thought upon thought upon thought.

And apropos thought upon thought: It goes without saying that we also greet the philosophers. But for them we need—above all—to pray that they get some sleep.

We (which is to say I) especially want to wish a Happy New Year to the women, because they so often go unloved. And of all of mankind's crimes, this is the greatest.

[153]

The reader should always see the paper that's behind the words. Not what was there before the words were written, but what resurfaces after they're read.

Don't believe the physicists who talk about specific density. Things that you see, even if they seem heavy, are all the stuff of dreams. And don't believe that either. The dream itself is a dream.

But wait. When you see large things like a hippopotamus or a Sumo wrestler you're tempted to credit them with an exaggerated degree of actuality. My stepmother Francesca, for instance, was very hard to doubt. But once we knew a very fragile woman, who appeared and then vanished like a hologram. It was very easy to doubt her, but the longing for her was painful.

[154]

Because of this longing, which is in fact hard to bear, novels of some three hundred and even six hundred pages are written and countless numbers of people who fill them come and go, like a medicine cabinet full of Tylenol.

You need to put things beside one another, a novel like this one and a crow. Or, if you'd rather, a turtle.

Once a crow came in through the front door and stood on the kitchen table. At first it pecked at breadcrumbs and then it froze there and stared at us.

That's why we're writing what we write. If only we knew what he saw when he stared we would tell the reader (instead of this book). But because we don't, we keep on writing.

[155]

Now we're reminded that a son was born to Uncle Shamu and his Muslim wife, and he was called Moshe. Maybe because both the Jews and the Muslims believe in the biblical Moses and maybe because his grandfather, which is to say, Uncle Shamu's father, was called Sandor Moshe Farkash.

Uncle Shamu and his Muslim wife are already dead and their son Moshe left for America and opened a refrigerator business there. We visited him when we were in New York. He lives in Queens, and his wife, who came from Croatia, made us latkes. As we said goodbye, Moshe hugged us and gave us a fountain pen. One of those pens that his father, Uncle Shamu, had left behind.

In Tel Aviv, at the last store that sells vintage fountain pens (on Allenby Street), they replaced the rubber ink sac, straightened the gold nib just a little, and sold us a new inkwell. Sometimes we dip the nib into the well, fill the pen with ink, then squirt the ink back out.

[156]

On this night (2009, between the third and fourth of January) the cannons are roaring and therefore the muses have to be silenced. In any case, they're infernal females who trouble the sleep of man.

All we can think of is the song we heard a long time ago, when we were little. Maybe Francesca, my stepmother, sang it. *O dear Augustin, Augustin, Augustin, O Augustin, my dear, all is lost.*

Uncle Max, my stepmother Francesca's father's brother, was taken by the Gestapo to a concentration camp. He clutched his World War I medals to his chest and hobbled along on his wooden leg (the leg of flesh he'd given as a gift to Germany) out to the street.

His leg most likely went up in smoke at Auschwitz. But if we had it today we'd set it afire now in order to warm up the people of Gaza, who are freezing.

[157]

Now that we've remembered the song about Augustin, we also remember the tongue twisters my stepmother Francesca taught us.

Try saying the following: "Der Potsdamer Postkutscher putzt den Potsdamer Postkutschekasten" (that is, approximately, the Potsdam post coach's coachman cleans the postbox of the post coach of Potsdam).

Or: "Herr von Hagen darf ich fra-gen, wie viel Kra-gen, Sie getra-gen, als Sie la-gen krank am Ma-gen in der Hauptstadt Kopenha-gen" (more roughly still, Dare I ask, Mr. von Hagen, / how tight was the collar you wore when you gagged on / the apple core, which left you sore, / in the capital's hospital, in Copenhagen).

Or (in Berlin German): "Ick sitze da und esse Klops, / uff eenmal kloppt's / ick denk nanu! Nanu denk ick / Ick jehe raus und kieke, / und wer steht draußen? Icke!"

(which says, more or less, I'm sitting and eating my supper, / and then there's a knock at the door— / Who is it, I wonder, who is it for? / So I go out to see— / and … who's standing there? / Me!).

[158]

And in fact, wherever you look you'll see yourself. And others too are only images on the screen that's you.

As a woman once said to us: What am I to you? When you look at me you see only yourself. And I'm here. Here. Here. That's what she said, and she pounded her fist against her heart.

Her name, that woman's, was Francine, and in the end she left us. She went back to her home in Quebec and became an English teacher. Now she's standing there and explaining the difference between the first person and the third person. If we'd known that difference then, we wouldn't have lost her.

[159]

Francine spoke Canadian French, which is like Yiddish in relation to German.

She bathed with two bars of soap and explained that each bar suited a different part of the body. Fine down sprouted along her legs and when the sun came up across them, it seemed as though the down was cast in gold.

We could write countless stories. "Francine on the Beach" (how the big toe of her right foot was cut by a piece of glass and she cried, "*Zut alors*") or "Francine on Shenkin Street" (how she tried on a pair of boots and removed them with a kick and one boot landed on the top shelf) or "Francine at the Café" (how she spilled her beer onto the pavement stone just to watch it fizz).

We don't know which sun comes up over Quebec and which moon lights up its night. Most likely a different sun and a different moon. But if it's the same sun that rises here and the same moon that lights our night I would write on them with two long brushes (a brush for day and a brush for night) "O Francine."

[160]

The reader can no doubt guess what sort of music we're trying to compose. Mostly blues. That sentimental melancholy suits us as a suit fits a tailor's dummy. If someone tells us to look at something rationally, in a major key— as, for instance, Telemann did—we get angry.

Take the shelves in the supermarket. They're trying to tempt us to process the arrangement of boxes and packages systematically. But we see cornflakes and think of snowflakes falling on the Siberian tundra, or we see soup mix and think of stardust.

Whoever understands these things can join the secret order whose members send one another signs by moving their pinkies ever so slightly. Look carefully. You'll find them, even at gatherings of the bar association.

Once we saw a man like that at the train station in Budapest and we fell all over him.

[161]

We've forgotten to tell our readers about our neighbors. Mr. Nahmias occasionally makes a swerving kicking motion. He's a fan of the Liverpool soccer team. The neighbor on the other side, Mr. Sapoznikov, goes up and down the stairs while reading *Globes*, the financial paper. Our Hello-how-are-you relations are much better with Mrs. Nahmias than they are with Mrs. Sapoznikov.

One floor down there's an architect whose name is Pnei-Gal, but we don't see him very often, because (so we've heard) he's an ecological architect. Which is to say, he designs houses that work in harmony with the earth and so on.

Pnei-Gal, the architect, is a very thin man with narrow shoulders, but we usually see only his back. Mr. Sapoznikov, on the other hand, who owns an excavation equipment company, usually comes at us head on, that is, from the front.

Of all the women in our entry we're partial to Mrs. Nahmias. Mrs. Sapoznikov looks too much like her husband, and the architect, Pnei-Gal, lives alone, or with another man.

We think this chapter's all confused, maybe because we don't really have a clear sense of our neighbors.

[162]

We won't talk about our immediate family in this book. We've already done that in another book, and there too we've concealed certain things. But between us, which is to say, ourselves and ourselves, we know that every word in it is dedicated to Nurit in lieu of a thousand bouquets of flowers.

What *can* be revealed is the view through the window. The mountain. What's in front of it and behind it and to its sides (and also above it) is always in motion. It alone stands there, as they say, immobile and silent.

And it has no name. And one can see it only as it is. And it can't be explained or criticized or made fun of.

We ask God's forgiveness for the fact that we've some-times (in distress) prayed to it. But we worship the mountain.

[163]

At the foot of the mountain there's a creek that dries up in summer and if you follow the water-worn pebbles and stones you'll get (after three miles) to a pool containing translucent fish.

We remember the legend about the city beneath Lake Baikal in Siberia. We saw how, during the winter, when the lake is frozen, people lie on its surface and look into it and sometimes they go back to their villages along the shore with a mysterious expression on their faces.

Some of them never leave their wooden homes. They sit all winter long and look out at other lakes, the ones at the bottom of their souls. In any event, anyone who sees the sunken city (outside or within) knows something that the others don't.

Imagine that they saw the sunken city and the world around it. And that they'd seen another lake. And people are also looking into that lake and seeing beneath it a sunken city wherein people are lying on the frozen sur-face of a lake and so on and on into infinity.

Once we knew a Russian man who, every morning (be-fore the sun came up), would walk a white dog. We said good morning to him and he always answered (with a Russian accent) "wolking."

[164]

We dream that a man (apparently us) buys a musical instru-ment, probably a mandolin or a Japanese koto for seventy-one thousand and several hundred (we don't know what currency) though the instrument isn't worth more than three hundred.

Leaping with joy, the two salesmen escape with the money to a place (apparently Rosh Pina) that's full of people and where it's hard to find a room for the night. In the end we pay four hundred (in that same currency) for a small, filthy room and then we wake up.

Generally speaking. Our behavior in dreams is irre-sponsible. The men expected no more than a few hun-dred. But we made some calculations on the tablecloth and proposed that astronomical sum ourselves.

At least we didn't commit any crimes in this dream. Sometimes we murder. But usually we fly high in the air and dream that others don't know how to fly, apart from one person who lives in Mevasseret Tziyon.

When we were little we understood one day (as we woke) that in fact (which is to say, in the waking world) we can't fly, and our hearts broke.

[165]

Now our readers no doubt understand why we can't continue the story we started (about Zivit and Ohad and so on). The gravitational field of that story is too strong. Even more so than the gravitational fields of physical bodies.

The readers can invite Zivit and Ohad (together or separately) for a cup of coffee. Then can ask them how they are and Zivit or Ohad (or both at once) will tell them.

Once we took a trip to London and saw, on Oxford Street, a character from one of the stories we'd written. We don't particularly like that story and have almost completely forgotten what it says there. But we remember that this character (we called him Gurnischt) married a British woman and settled in London.

This movement between two worlds is imaginary. After all, someone is writing us as well. Someone is reading us. And someone is having critical thoughts. And someone is filing us away.

It's the dentists who teach us which world is more real.

When we were little they sent us to Dr. Buchstabe, who lived (oddly) on Child's Boulevard, behind the Ordeo Cinema in Ramat Gan. Dr. Buchstabe operated the drill by pressing a pedal with his right foot, just as they operated sewing machines at the time.

Dr. Buchstabe had a peculiar sense of humor. Before starting the drill (there were, we recall, also leather straps involved in the mechanism), he'd ask: Do you think it will hurt? The terrible pain caused by that mechanical drill taught us about history (the Inquisition, etcetera) better than any teacher ever did.

In Dr. Buchstabe's waiting room there were pictures of famous dentists, but then again maybe they were just his ancestors, and the pungent smell that hung in the air would have driven away any and all thoughts of madeleines from Proust.

When they told us that Dr. Buchstabe had died we remembered the story about the man who heard that Edison (who invented the light bulb) had died and thought that from that day on darkness would reign in the world.

But after Dr. Buchstabe's death, dentists continued to drill in our mouths. And now their drills ran on electricity.

[167]

How sad the days of childhood are. Everyone else is bigger and ugly and they're always talking about the upper level of things. The bus is coming. It's six o'clock. The curtain is dirty, etcetera.

They go up and down stairs. And enter and exit through doors, wearing all the while a practical expression, of the sort one sees on a taxi dispatcher.

None of them ever say, We're going from here to there on the face of a planet, and the planet itself is spinning in a great darkness that has no end.

What could we do? The other children were bigger than we were as well, every time, apart from one girl, whom we suspected (mistakenly) might also have known about the planet and the darkness.

[168]

Today (January 8, 2009) the enemy attacked the Zilberman Residential Hotel in Nahariya (which is also called the Golden Age Home).

In the confusion, Rivkah Leibowitz (age eighty-six) pushed her wheelchair to the street and turned toward Ga'aton Boulevard. She crossed the road to the south side and rolled her chair into the Penguin Café.

There she ordered a deluxe breakfast (though she'd already had her hard-boiled egg and cream of wheat at the Zilberman) and took a woman's magazine from the newspaper stand.

First she read a long article about women who fake orgasm. Then a feature about the singer Sarit Hadad, and finally letters from readers (I'm thirty-six, my husband is a good man and a devoted father to our two children but).

When she was done with her breakfast (only half of the tuna spread was left on her tray) she wheeled herself west, toward the shore, and there she sat, beneath the crows, looking out at the great body of water.

[169]

In the end the sun set and another calibration began (maybe the ninth of the month). Other things happened in other places. We could write that men were killed there and there people died, and there they were born— but these things are understood.

All this trouble of writing a book and printing a book and selling a book and reading a book and translating a book is a waste of time unless, in the end, it brings people joy.

And so, the past has already been. The future isn't yet with us, and the present is only a future becoming a past. Joy? In what? Maybe in that the past has already been and the future is yet to come and the present can be either. Which is to say, that everything's nothing.

There is no greater delight than that, since, if we look around us, the nothing is packed to the rafters.

[170]

As for war. They should call up reserves of literary critics. They'd vanquish the enemy with their weighty pronouncements. Afterward, the critics could enlist the lethal forces of verbal contortion and extensive annotation to verify that the enemy in fact had been crushed. Imagine the shock of (for instance) religious fanatics in the face of *that* technology.

There's also a chance that, confronted with their sudden and frightening appearance on the battlefield, the enemy would simply experience a conversion and throw itself at their feet.

Which reminds us of Mrs. Unger, whom we once knew, when we lived in Haifa.

Usually Mrs. Unger was a very soft woman. She baked pecan cookies and poppy-seed cookies and read romance novels in Hebrew and in Hungarian.

But sometimes, maybe once every two months, she'd wave her right hand in the air (without moving the rest of her body) and slap her husband.

No wonder Mr. Unger always moved in such wide circles around his wife.

[171]

We miss poetry. Yesterday we read a poem in *Ha'aretz* about a swan that falls into the water and we too are trying to bring down a swan. But the swans get away and the sea is full of battleships.

Maybe one should begin artificially, without inspiration, and then inspiration will follow. Since now it's night and everyone's sleeping we could start with "The city breathes in chloroform." Except that we've heard that chloroform hasn't been used for ages in operating rooms, and we don't know what sort of anesthesia they use today.

Maybe one needs to think about a single detail and not an entire city. Pertaining to Mr. Yellinek, for instance. On the face of it, there's nothing poetic about Mr. Yellinek. But in fact, when he opens his mailbox day after day it's impossible to look directly at him, just as one can't stare at the sun (Mr. Yellinek is five feet three inches tall and barely reaches the mailbox) without going blind.

[172]

And there's nothing more poetic than notes from the housing committee (each person owes such and such).

Or an antenna. But then you're tempted to put birds on it and that ruins the poem. Generally. Whatever seems like a poem isn't a poem and what doesn't seem like a poem is.

Tiberias, for example, is full of poems. Also Afula. And Birmingham. Especially the hotel where we got a room for twenty pounds a night but had to climb over the beds to get to the shower.

We've already talked about phone books. Under "H" we find our name among others, and look at it (that is, at the name) and at the number beside it and don't understand.

All these things (that is, not putting birds on the antenna and not understanding our name) are necessary conditions for poetry. But not sufficient. Something else is needed. Perhaps a great sadness or maybe great joy. Or quiet.

[173]

Maybe this quiet we long for is a sign that the book is nearing its end. We're not sure.

Maybe from here on in we need to do what Joyce did in his final book and write in a kind of parallel language.

Something like O my mother in Hinfich feel phaned a slanguage a slanguage and more. Piraeus isn't far. And the stubbledom oh the stubbledom. My mother whom our mother recovers the sea covers the great sees and more across unto pain extends to the end to the end. And if and mother and father and rivers and rivers oh no once again and again, oh since she has a very great ball and a dress made of others and a wonder and brother and canals of algae and cruel stubbling like a knife that our father that very same knife and a glinting or glash. O my mother the willow the bowl.

And so on. But there's no escaping in that direction. Why not? This our readers understand quite well on their own.

[174]

After he'd written like that, Joyce wrote no more. When they asked him why, he answered roughly as follows: I'll write only if I find very simple words, very very simple words.

We know some simple words. For example: "There once was a rabbit / who had the bad habit / of twitching the end of his nose. / His sisters and brothers / and various others / said, 'Look at the way he goes!'"

Not a superfluous word. And one can see it all. The rabbit. The field he's looking for food in. His sensitive nose. And it gets better:

"But one little bunny / said 'Isn't it funny' / and practiced it down in the dell. / Said the others 'If *he* can, / I'm certain that *we* can,' / and they all did it rather well! // Now all the world over, / where rabbits eat clover / And dig and scratch with their toes, / Each little rabbit / has got the bad habit / of twitching the end of his nose!"

If only we could write like that.

Or the way that Louis Armstrong sang. Come to think of it, he too twitched his nose.

[175]

At some point along the way (maybe when we were infants even) something got scrambled and we started putting words on top of each other (and not side by side).

At school for sure. Louis Armstrong couldn't read music. Why did they send us there? After all, we could already talk.

On the board the teacher wrote "Shalom, first grade," but we cried. A woman came and said my name is Tzipporah and we wanted our mother. Why did they make us sit in chairs and tell us that we couldn't move?

When we gave things names we did so as though in a dream. But then they forced us to give the names letters, and that was too much. They placed bright lights directly before us, as though the sun weren't enough. Why did they make us sit in those chairs?

Then came the sin of addition. How much is such and such plus such and such? Before that we were never wrong. Only afterward did we start to make mistakes.

[176]

The first-grade chairs became computer chairs. Now we're sitting in front of large screens, our face is pale and our spine is bent, and we send each other odd signs.

Sometimes the computers crash and entire love stories vanish. Addresses can't be recovered and the faces aren't yet known.

Stricken with sorrow, people head into the streets, carrying clumps of metal in their hands, but the technicians aren't able to get the names and phone numbers out of them, and since the people have lost the power of speech, they withdraw into themselves, like that gray worm that shrivels up when you touch it.

Today the storks are coming to mothers giving birth. Each beak bears a small computer, and the whole world has been destroyed by a blackout.

[177]

Yesterday Mr. Yellinek asked Mr. Nahmias (the Liverpool fan) to lower his mailbox.

First, Mr. Nahmias removed the box from the wall. He leaned it against the stairwell wall and went to get a drill.

When he returned he asked Mr. Yellinek: Where do you want it? Mr. Yellinek made an arc-like motion with his hand (as though he were opening an imaginary mailbox) and said: Here.

Mr. Nahmias drilled a hole where Mr. Yellinek had indicated and, with light taps from his hammer, he inserted a plastic dowel into the hole. With the help of a screwdriver, into the dowel he turned a large screw, on which he hung the mailbox.

Mr. Yellinek said Thank you very much and (because his head reached only to the chest of Mr. Nahmias) held out his hand toward Mr. Nahmias's private parts. Mr. Nahmias shook the hand and said: It's nothing. Then he gathered up the drill and the hammer and the screwdriver and the toolbox and went back to his apartment. Mr. Yellinek, on the other hand, stood there in front of his mailbox for a good long while.

[178]

In a previous life Mr. Yellinek was, no doubt, a pony and the mailbox a bale of hay or a water trough.

We'd like to come back as a bakery. As all that's in it. As ovens. Fire. Loaves. So that our soul would become the soul of a bakery.

But our karma will undoubtedly take us in another direction. Most likely we'll become a vole. Or, what's it called? A broker (that is, on the stock market). Or a tragic historical figure.

Sometimes (mostly in dreams) we see something from our past lives. We were a pumpkin salesman at a market in Europe during the time of the Black Death or a Roman senator during the war with Carthage.

Once we had a nightmare. That we'd been reincarnated as ourselves and everything was happening for a second time. Step by step and word by word exactly as it had happened in our life, including our shoe size (9 $^1/_2$).

That's why we like the way Jews bury their dead. The shrouds through which one can see the outline of the body. The sound of the corpse hitting the bottom of the hole. The prayer El Malei Rahamim—God, full of mercy. That absolute end and return to dust.

[179]

And that's why happiness ascends from, of all places, cemeteries. No order is finer than that of those rows upon rows. And especially the great quiet, sometimes with just the sound of a hoe against the soil or the call of a crow.

Life itself should be lived like that. As in a silent film in which one sees only a single hut with a rooster strutting every so often from the left side of the screen toward the right, and a little while later coming back across it.

Once every thousand years or so a word will be heard. Like the sound of very distant thunder. A word like *zoo* or *zero* or *zillion*. Words, that is, which start with the final letter.

In this world there won't be any information at all. That is, it won't be possible to store anything. Memory will be something else entirely. More like a pane of transparent glass. And matter? Whatever you'd like it to be. But endless. One thing within another.

On second thought, even that word is superfluous. Perhaps the sound is sufficient. Something like the "A" that a tuning fork makes when the string instruments are being tuned. But only the "A." Without the program or the concert that follows.

[180]

We've come to death and even to life that resembles death and the book's still going on.

Maybe because we like to drink a certain kind of sherry. Not the kind they import to Israel, but another one. If we could remember what it was called, we'd ask our wine store to bring us a case of it.

We don't want to say banal things about people we love, etcetera. We just want to say something about the wondrous nature of the heart. The muscle itself. That it's stretched and contracted some seventy times a minute sixty minutes each hour and twenty-four hours a day three hundred and sixty-five days a year for maybe eighty years, and only the wizards of arithmetic can figure out how many beats that makes.

And, because we're grateful to this muscle, wherever it comes from and wherever it's going, it's forbidden for us to die before our time and we need to observe all the commandments in the proper manner, such as, for instance, the one concerning the sherry.

And if we remember the name of that wine we'll insist that the publisher order maybe eighty cases and distribute the bottles to bookstores, so that the readers can taste it.

[181]

We'd like to share all sorts of things with our readers. Not just wine.

For example, in Japanese, the syllable *ka* is like a question mark. You say something like "We're going to Tokyo tomorrow." But if you add a *ka* to the end of the sentence, the meaning changes to "Are we going to Tokyo tomorrow?"

The reader can read books that way. That is, as though there were a *ka* at the end of every sentence. The book would then be a long series of questions (among others about the sun and the moon and the stars) and we could call it *The Book of Great Doubt*. We could even call it *The Book of Tremendous Doubt* if we added the *ka* to the end of every word. But there's no need to go that far.

In fact, faith is preferable to doubt. It's better to read the book as though there were an exclamation mark at the end of every sentence. Or better still, as though each sentence were followed by those three letters that religious Jews are always adding to everything—*bet, samekh, dalet* (which stand for "with the help of God")—and then we could call it *The Book of Great Faith*.

Imagine putting *bet, samekh, dalet* before every sentence and *ka* at its end. Then what?

[182]

These things are linked to Mr. Yellinek. We didn't count him as one of our neighbors and then (when Mr. Nahmias fixed his mailbox for him) we spoke of him as though he were one.

The reader might ask himself: Is Mr. Yellinek a neighbor or not? Or worse, he could ask himself if Mr. Yellinek even exists.

But this is a question that shouldn't be asked. Everyone exists. Especially Mrs. Shtiasny and her Italian husband. If you start casting doubt on this or that character you'll need, at the end of the day, to doubt the existence of all the characters—even the author himself (that is, Yoel Hoffmann), and worse still, yourself.

And so, Mr. Yellinek exists exactly as Mrs. Shtiasny exists and as her Italian husband exists. You can see him here and there (mostly in Tel Aviv) standing in front of mailboxes.

Generally speaking. The word *exists* is an ugly word. At most it might suit a kind of screw but not all of creation. And if our readers insist on using it, they should at least write it with a *ks* instead of an *x*.

[183]

January two thousand and nine. During the war we inhale the air that we exhale and not new air. Our dark father, who stands behind our biographical father, gives birth to us.

In this way too mankind goes astray. It gathers up information all the time like a mad quartermaster, but during a war even the mad go mad.

When we were soldiers we never managed to get things straight and polish what was supposed to be polished. Our steel helmet rocked from side to side, our backpack slipped off of our shoulders, our canteen got dirty, and the rifle was never properly calibrated. Our dark father accompanied us wherever we went and our mother was far away or dead.

There was always someone very short (shorter even than Mr. Yellinek) who made everyone laugh. Mostly his name was Yirmiyahu but everyone called him Yirmi and every once in a while Yahu. What was so funny about him? For instance, he stuffed his ammunition pouch not with extra rounds but with cans of sardines and slabs of cheese. He was the one who'd light the fire and then piss on the coals before we left. Everyone had a girlfriend (or everyone said they did) and he was the only one who didn't. But he had some thingamajig that he loved. A pocketknife or a large marble or a pen on which a naked woman rose and fell.

[184]

The German word for war is *krieg*, and it's a word that suits a kind of cracker (or rusk) and not the shedding of blood. Francesca, my stepmother, sometimes said *krieg* but, because of her build, it sounded different.

Generally, a word depends on who says it. Think, for example, of the philosopher Yeshayahu Leibowitz and Mary, the Holy Virgin. We're having a hard time thinking of a word that both might have uttered, but it's clear that if they said that word, in each case we'd imagine something completely different.

Once we knew a woman who wanted a child very badly but miscarried every one she conceived. She sat in cafés and so on, like everyone, but every time—roughly once a year—when they asked her (and also when they didn't), she'd say: The baby died.

Correct. The baby would have died in any case. He'd have died in a war or of old age. And so it's possible to say such a thing about every baby. But that he died before she managed to see him. And that he died before he managed to see her. And that afterward she sat in cafés and had to say those words. All these things are harder even than war to bear.

[185]

We should seat Mr. Yellinek (and Yirmiyahu from the army) on the backs of wild geese, so they can fly far above the earth like Nils Holgersson.

We'll have to say goodbye to them as they're going beyond the borders of the book. Wild geese don't comply with literary convention. But they'll hover in other worlds and from a great height see the well-tended fields and the places where people live. They won't be able to see people from that height, and so the journey will involve a certain amount of loneliness. But imagine that the heavens are one huge mailbox and letters arrive for Mr. Yellinek from distances that he can't fathom.

We could end the book like that, but most of our characters are too heavy to put on the backs of wild geese. We ourselves (which is to say, I) would like to leave the book that way. And, if possible, the world—period. But some inexplicable stubbornness is compelling us to get at least to chapter 200 and, if possible (though this in fact is beyond our control), to our eightieth year.

[186]

We know some professors who are the exact opposite of wild geese.

First of all, they're always quarreling and therefore they can't take off and fly in those beautiful formations. Second, their colors. They're never white. Usually they're one shade or another of green or yellow. Third, their necks are short.

And there's another difference. Wild geese leave no traces. If you say that they're here, they're there. If you say that they're there, you've lost them. Professors, on the other hand, never move from their positions. Moreover, they draw everything to where they are. Soup. Various items. Gravitational fields, etcetera. Many are like a German housewife who's always pickling cucumbers.

Though now we'll risk being sued for libel, we'll mention in particular Professor Har-Shoshanim (formerly Rosenberg). You'll always find him opening doors or shutting them. He wears brown leather shoes and you'll never catch him with both of his feet in the air. When he speaks what he says is all too clear and others, therefore (others, that is, in his proximity), need to take Prozac. Above all, he's an associate professor and in the end will become (unlike the wild geese) a full professor.

[187]

Once Professor Har-Shoshanim proposed during a faculty meeting that two departments be merged and two others be split. His hands made a motion indicating a merger (when he spoke of merging) and another one suggesting a split (when he spoke of splitting).

It's very hard to remember the reasoning that he laid out for the council. But we remember the gold frames of his glasses glinting in the neon light. Maybe his rivals were thinking (as in the stories by Karl May about the Indians and the eclipse) that the glinting indicated hidden powers. In any event, his proposal for the merger (and for the split) were approved by a large majority.

In the parking lot, next to his Mazda Lentis, Professor Har-Shoshanim took off his glasses and wiped the lenses. He stood there, alone, his head rising like a disk over the cars of the senior faculty.

There are moments in human history that have to be given a name. That moment will most likely be called "the moment when Har-Shoshanim took off his glasses" or "the moment when Har-Shoshanim looked toward the university but didn't see it."

[188]

Imagine the loneliness of writers surrounded by the characters from all their books and unable to get away from them and go back to their families.

There's no consolation to be had from Har-Shoshanim. We tried going to his home and couldn't. We tried to meet him in the cafeteria. Again, no luck.

With Mr. Yellinek we manage to get along, somehow. We can pay him our dues for the housing board (thirty shekels) and offer him a cup of tea. But then he goes silent. We need someone we can talk to, but can't find anyone like that in the entire book (apart from the dead, of course).

The girls we had crushes on are already old (in the book as well) and if we had a friend or two we wouldn't want to see them if they were older than seventy or so. What would we talk about. Arthritis?

Maybe it's our problem. We're anti-social, and so at best we live in peace with an imaginary notion of women.

[189]

But it isn't right to trouble our readers with these sorts of things. If we're not mistaken, we also promised (in the opening chapter) a love story.

If we're afraid of close quarters we can find it (love, that is) in large train stations. Sit on a bench in the main concourse and think of the high ceiling as the dome of heaven and the people coming and going as creatures of God. Regina and Moshe and Shalom (with the suitcases). And Odelia. And Haim. And Mr. Schwartz, whose hair has gone white. And the entire Na'im family (with the elderly aunt). And Abramov. Who *isn't* there?

You can go up to them as though you were the Pope in the great square and open your arms wide as though you were a fisher of men. And whoever comes into them comes into them. And deserves love.

And don't be put off by the fear in people's faces. And don't worry about the policeman who might take you away. You can embrace him as well. And, above all, don't lose that love when you're with the psychiatrist they'll quickly call in. It isn't his fault. Just tell him: You too are worthy. You too.

[190]

We'd like to leave our readers with a great gift before they move on to other books. Perhaps a character. But we're like a building contractor whose tools are limited. At most he puts up a wall or lays down a floor and says to the client that he should use his imagination to fill in the rest.

Assume for a moment that the criminal code applied to writers as well. We would be sued for negligence and the incompletion of characters just as suits are brought against contractors.

Your honor, we'd say, but we've given the reader the essential quality in each case. There is no such thing, the judge would reply, the reader's entitled to all the particulars.

Once we knew a woman whom we could describe (on our own) down to the last of the thousands of hairs on her head. That's how much care we took with her character. But if we were to do that now, our readers would sue us for excessive particularity.

So all we can offer our readers is this: a large mug with the words GOOD MORNING (in English) written across it. They can drink their morning coffee from it and picture a person in their mind's eye.

[191]

In addition to the mug (as in a buy-one-get-one-free special) we could tell a beautiful tale:

In the beginning, when God was creating the heaven and the earth, the earth was formless and waste, and darkness was over the face of the deep, and a wind from God hovered over the face of the waters.

Imagine the loneliness of countless years. Like a giant, old autistic man, He stared into what was and saw not even a crack. And because of its tremendous proportions, not even an angle or a curve. And when He looked outside, on account of His great pain, He saw only something like a cloud or pale washes of color. How long could He remain like that, all alone?

The only consolation was His name (or, more accurately, His names). But when He uttered them, He heard (because of the absolute emptiness) not even an echo.